THE Dragon Bone JOURNAL

2026 ISSUE

Copyright Page

TRIGGER WARNINGS:

Child Harm

THE 2026 ISSUE

THE
DRAGON BONE
JOURNAL

COMPILED BY
SERA AMOROSO

Escape With Us

Look no further for your next favorite book!

This year we're proud to compare a few of our most popular titles with other amazing books so you can find your next favorite read! Each comes highly recommended from Nathaniel Luscombe and Effie Joe Stock.

Our Top Three Dragon Bone Approved Book Comparisons of 2026

HUMAN SCARS ON PLANET SKIN BY EFFIE JOE STOCK & NATHANIEL LUSCOMBE &

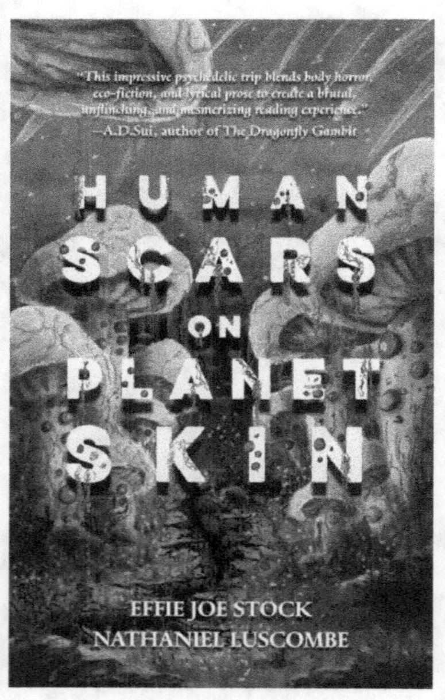

Do you love reading strange science fiction where the main character isn't human? Then Human Scars on Planet Skin and Landlocked in Foreign Skin will quickly become your next book obsessions. Both offer a unique spin on science fantasy, puttin the reader in the minds and bodies of creatures living in opposition to humans. While exploring the horror of being trapped in a fragile body made of flesh, both of these books also explore themes of culture erasure and the intense drive to find individuality in a crumbling world.

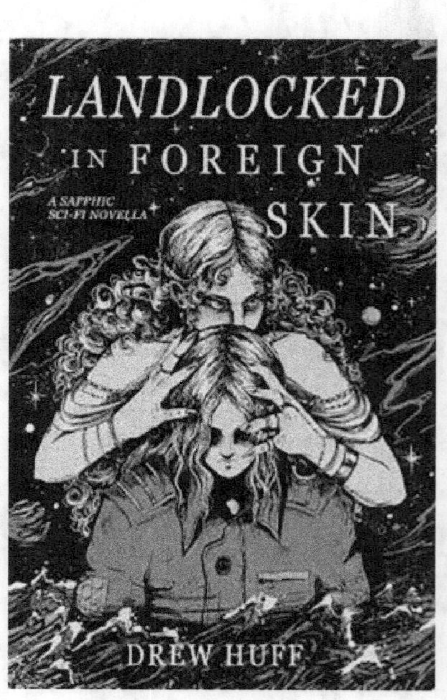

SHARED TROPES:
Alien/Colonization Horror
Body Horror
Non-Human MC
Human Corpse Consumption
Trauma Rep

THE AWAKENING OF LORA ABERNATHY BY MJ ANTHONY & HOWL BY SHAUN DAVID HUTCHINSON

What do The Awakening of Lora Abernathy by MJ Anthony and Howl by Shaun David Hutchinson have in common? They're both werewolf-coded stories that dive deep into identity, found family, love, and being queer. If you want your heart to be softly crushed by speculative stories that feel almost real, these stories will deliver. They're the perfect read for anyone trying to find their place in this harsh world.

THISTLEHEART HOME BY R.C. LLOYD & INSTRUCTIONS FOR TRAVELING WEST BY JOY SULLIVAN

If you enjoy stories told through poetry, you'd love ThistleHeart Home by R.C. Lloyd and Instructions for Traveling West by Joy Sullivan. While these appear to be quite different on the outside, they hold a lot of similarities at their core. ThistleHeart Home is about a girl wandering through the dark woods. Instructions for Traveling West is about Joy wandering through life. One is a more fictionalized version, but both are based heavily on truth, as most poetry is. With writing vivid enough to paint pictures, these collections will leave you begging for more.

All the Exciting 2026 Updates for Dragon Bone Publishing

Dragon Bone Publishing was born out of a dream of passion. Passion for writing, reading, learning, and for life itself. Believing everything has a deeper meaning and complexity than often explored, Dragon Bone Publishing seeks to expose the depth and intricacy of the world around us using the words of multi-faceted authors, the magic and mystery of epic fantasy, the science and possibility of sci-fi, the symbolism and truths of allegory, and the wonder of a child's mind.

Submissions Are Open!

Want to be published by us? Submissions for the Journal are open!

THE
DRAGON BONE
JOURNAL
2027 ISSUE

Our mission at Dragon Bone Publishing™ is to encourage authors with their passions by publishing their writing, offering tools and tricks of the trade, and spreading the word about their work! What better way to do that than a magazine?

Want to get in on the action in the 2027 Issue of the Dragon Bone Journal? Submissions open January 1st, 2026!
For more information and the submission form, visit:
www.dragonbonepublishing.com

All of our titles are available internationally, through our local distrubution channels and/or on our website www.dragonbonepublishing.com/shop

HUMAN SCARS ON PLANET SKIN BY EFFIE JOE STOCK & NATHANIEL LUSCOME

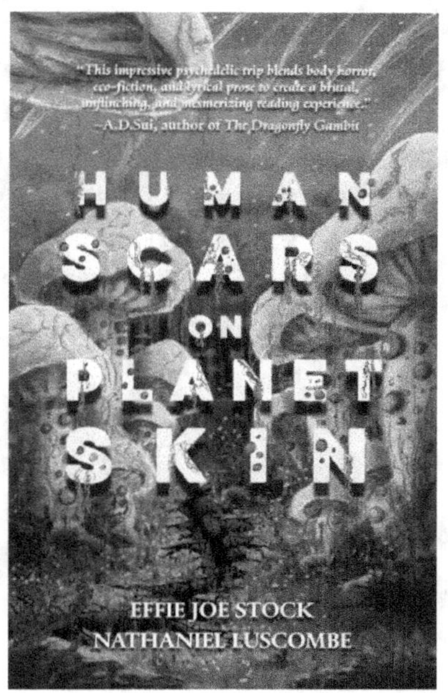

Turr is fighting back for what was stolen from her: her body and her children living on it.

After the humans tried to colonize her, Turr was forced to resort to mass violence to reclaim her skin. But in fleeing the planet, the humans left behind a chemical disaster—the dead zone.

To bring peace and life back to herself, Turr sends out a desperate plea to two shroom people: Invidia and Clyra. Invidia, though surrounded by death, is tasked with learning how to breathe life back into the land. Clyra must lead a group of broken failed experiments through the forest, following a trail of visions. Death and uncertainty face them at every turn, but only when they're all together can the planet truly begin to heal.

THE AWAKENING OF LORA ABERNATHY BY MJ ANTHONY

After a disastrous birthday ceremony and coming-of-age ritual gone wrong, Lora flees home, taking her new lycanthrope form for a test drive on the streets of Glenhurst, and hoping to prove her worth. When she answers a local job posting at random, Lora lands in the company of two other strangers: Nic and Art.

Nic has sought redemption from his own past failings on his fiancé's family farm. When that security is threatened, he takes matters into his own hands, seeking out a connection from his sister's college days, who is rumored to have experience with magic blades and killing tyrants.

Art longs for the past about as often as he longs to forget it, pouring his time into cooking, mutual aid efforts, bounty hunting gig work, and studying crosscosm theory (the idea of travel between worlds). This job will pay his rent, and, if he's lucky, not give him time to think about his trauma.

The job? Enter the forest and eliminate the threat that's been causing townsfolk and travelers to go missing. But the woods are dark, and they have eaten adventurers before. When their pasts come back to haunt them, can the fledgling party survive?

Aphotic Love
An Anthology on the Depths of Romance

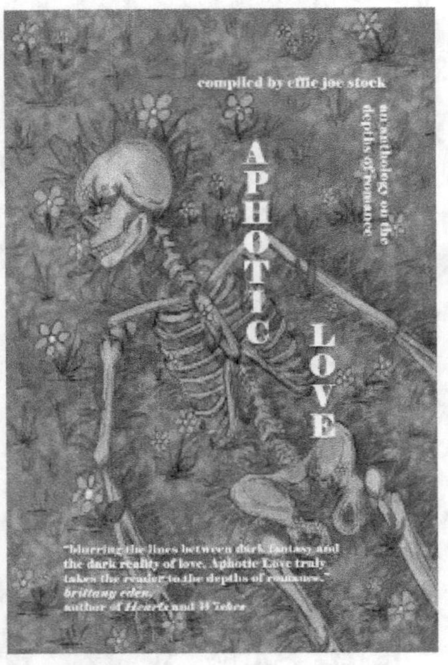

Love is often depicted as light, joyful, fun, exciting, or carefree. But a darker side to love lurks under the surface-a frightening, desperate, tragic side.

From the love of gods and goddesses, to mortals who fell in love with death. From pure sweet romance gone astray, to villains who loved the hero. An actress no longer acting she's in love, a phoenix whose lover gives everything to be with her reborn, a lonely queen whose touch turns loved ones to ice, a space station caught between the pain of two lovers.

Dare to dive deep into this raw, emotional collection of short stories, prose, and poems which strives to expose the lightless side of tragedy, heartbreak, desperation, and love.

Unconventional Love
An Anthology on the Expanse of Love

Familial. Romantic. Platonic.

Love is but one word struggling to encompass a wide variety of emotions, connections, relationships. This anthology seeks to sail the vastness of love's expanse and discover all the many ways humans love and are loved.

From loving your partner as a worm, to a love letter from a daughter to mother, to faun and mergirl lovers separated by culture, to a telepathic friendship nearly cast away, Unconventional Love is a collection like no other, bringing together hearts and emotions scattered across a universe so fast and an even greater love.

Upcoming Releases

THE WAYWARD SOULS
OF AVALON
BY A.L. DAVIDSON

Love spans farther than the most distant star and deeper than the darkest ocean.

After the collapse of Earth sends the last of humanity soaring to Mars, documentarian Jocasta Thorne finds himself trapped in his spaceship on the outskirts of the planet's orbit. Nearly giving up hope of ever seeing another human again, Jocasta's quiet life is disrupted when a knock at the bay door breaks through the silence, and the stranger on the other side promises he can get them home. The Wayward Souls of Avalon is a cozy sci-fi tale about two strangers caught in each other's orbits and their year-long trip to Mars, perfect for fans of Becky Chambers and "The Darkness Outside Us".

ASH BLACK
AND THE SEVEN WOLVES
BY EFFIE JOE STOCK

After the mysterious death of her father the king, Ash Black finds herself facing a growing evil amidst her hasty coronation. Whispered rumors of treason become a grim reality when her stepmother accuses her of wielding black magic and murdering the king, and announces that her own daughter, Snow White, will rise to the throne instead.

Her title stripped, wolf familiar torn from her side, and childhood love betrothed to her hateful half-sister, Ash Black awaits her trial in the forgotten depths of her castle. There, in a place so devoid of warmth, love, and light, Ash Black learns her communion with the night and the creatures who hide within are not just delusion, but a deep, powerful magic that has ruled the land for centuries.

With the help of a soul trapped in a mirror, a clever jumping spider, and seven wolf spirits, Ash Black races against time to awaken the magic within herself, bending darkness, blood, and bone to her will to destroy a light-ridden lie squeezing the balance and freedom from her kingdom. Yet as her lover, family, magic, and kingdom hang in the balance, Ash Black quickly finds no happy endings are won without immense sacrifice.

Dragon Heart Press

Poetry Imprint

2025 Releases

Instagram @dragon.heart.press
or
www.dragonbonepublishing.com/dragonheartpress

2026 Dragon Heart Press Releases

BENEATH THE TOWERING GARDENS OF BABYLON
BY JOY REDCEDARS

Bitter and hopeful, ugly and perfect, violent and tender and vast—this collection grasps at endless oppositions, weaving between the construction of an impossible tower to heaven and the devastating realities of public works.

Beneath the Towering Gardens of Babylon is the autobiography of a gardener and the grounds she tends. What fates may befall them? Are they truly as inescapable as she believes? How do we tell our stories under the shadow of our own destruction?

A LEASHED DESIRE TO FLEE
BY MYKA SILBER

Written over nearly two decades, the semi-autobiographical poems of A Leashed Desire to Flee reflect the anxieties of late teenagehood, the struggles of navigating adult life in their twenties, and the maturity and melancholy of their early thirties. This collection is a love song to anyone who has felt trapped in their life, longing to break through the bars of their cage.

A Hammer
to the Void
by Michelle Bulsiewicz

I have a degree in journalism and previously wrote and edited for the Deseret News. My book reviews, author interviews, and other articles are available to read at deseret.com. I am also an alumna of Adrienne Young's Writing With the Soul, a certified yoga instructor, and a lover of tea, cats, and the beach.

CW: child harm

The first message from my missing son came when I took a sledgehammer to the wall of my bathroom.

We'd been slowing remodeling our 1950s home since we moved in, when my son was born, working room by room. As he learned to take his first steps, we put new cabinets in the kitchen. As he memorized the letters of the alphabet, we tore out the carpet in the basement. As he grew and changed, so did this house.

Then one morning when he was seven years old I went into his room and he was gone. At first I thought he was hiding.

"Evander!" I called, his name riding on a laugh.

But as silence continued to meet my cries, as minutes wore on and every room stood empty of his mischievous giggles, my panic pressed against my chest until it burst.

Within the hour we called the police. The search started with the neighborhood and expanded to the city, then the country. There had been no sign of a struggle, of a kidnapping, of a ransom note. No woods or rivers or cliffs by our suburban home for him to get lost in. As time passed and the inevitability of finding only his corpse became horrifically apparent before our eyes—still we were met with only silence. Only his lack.

I could not function. I could not work. I could not socialize. I could only obsess over the lack of my son.

And I could destroy.

So, I picked up a sledgehammer and rammed it into the outdated bright pink tile of our second floor bathroom and only then did I find the first sign of my son.

Scratched into the wood beams—the bones of our house laid bare in the torn out guts of the shower wall—was the unmistakable scrawl of my small boy just learning how to write: MOM.

The letters had a harried slant, as if written in a rush, a lengthened, crooked line at the end of the last M, dashed off before he could really finish. I knew Evander had written it. It couldn't be anyone else.

Joe wasn't so sure. "No one's touched the inside of these walls in almost seventy years. Some little boy must have vandalized it back when they first built the place."

"But look at it. That's Evander's handwriting."

The look Joe gave me—pain and pity and frustration all jumbled into one in the creases between his brows.

"I want to find him too, Mariam, but pretending he's somehow writing inside our walls—that's not going to bring him back." His voice cracked on the words and he looked away, hiding his grief. Evander's disappearance was the wedge in the middle of the stream of our relationship, diverting our paths in opposite directions.

So, I stopped talking to Joe about Evander's messages but I didn't stop believing in them. And I didn't stop finding them.

Three days later I found another etched into the cement beneath the laminate floor: HELP. The same handwriting. The same hurried slant.

He was in trouble. He needed me. I didn't know how it was possible, but I didn't care. My search became desperate.

The next day a third message appeared on the back of the mirror when I pried it off the wall with a crow bar, the words painted in an unsightly rust red: FIND ME.

"I'm trying, baby," I whispered.

Joe walked in then and stared at the paint dried in cascading drips of red. Horror bottomed out in the depths of his pupils. "Mariam, is that…is that blood?"

I bit my lip. "I don't know. Maybe."

"You don't know?" He shook his head, pulling at his hair in agitation. "Are you—are you doing this? Is this some kind of sick playacting?"

"No, it's him." I thrust my arms toward the mirror on the floor. Fear constricted my throat, my voice coming out high-pitched and shrill. "He's trying to reach us."

"You need help, Mariam. This has gone too far."

I ignored him and picked up the sledgehammer.

"What are you doing?"

"I need to see if there's more." I slammed the hammer down on the bathroom counter top that broke away from the wall with a satisfying crack.

Joe backed away, hands held out in front of him. "I can't watch you do this." He turned and all but ran from me. I heard the front door slam with finality.

Fine. If he wouldn't believe me, I didn't need him. I could do this myself.

The image of my sweet boy, lost somewhere, somewhere no one could reach him, wounding himself just for the chance to communicate with me—it infused an urgency in my veins I could not strain out.

I threw the hammer harder and harder until the entire cabinet came off the wall. Then I demolished the cabinet to bits. Then I smashed into the wall, the floor, the toilet. Water burst from the pipes, soaking me to the skin, but I hardly noticed.

I could hear him. The indistinct sound of my son's voice as if from a distance, distorted by static, growing louder with every hurdle I destroyed. It reverberated in my brain, building pressure against my skull, hot and intense. Finally I could make out the words.

"Mommy, come get me. It's got me, Mommy. Save me. I'm here, Mommy. I'm right here."

"I'm coming, buddy. I've got you. Mommy's here." At some point tears began running in heavy rivulets down my chin and neck, unheeded, indistinct from the water spraying across the room. My vision blurred as I flew like a tornado through that bathroom, ripping apart everything in my path, everything between me and my baby boy.

"Mommy. Mommy. Mommy." His panicked voice grew louder. Closer. Closer. I could see him. Was that him in the window? What should have been a hazy view of the side of our neighbor's house through frosted glass, bright in the midday sun, had turned dark and opaque. I could just make out the smudged outline of a small child's hand banging against the barrier.

A niggling sense of reality tugged at the back of my brain. How could my seven-year-old, missing for weeks, somehow be outside my second-story bathroom window? Somehow this, not the messages buried inside the walls, not the disembodied voices, brought me my first moment of true doubt in my own sanity. I wished, for the first time, that Joe had stayed so I could go to him and make sure he could see this too.

"Mommy!" A tormented scream splintered through the glass. Fingers of darkness wrapped around the small hand at the window, dragging it away.

There was no time to decide what was real. My child was afraid. My child was in danger. I could only act.

Hefting the sledgehammer in my hands I swung it at the glass. It shattered beneath the force of my adrenaline.

Before my eyes, I saw my child's mop of brown hair, his freckled rounded face, his ragged, dirt encrusted fingernails, his pupils flared wide and fathomless, his mouth open in a great scream. A writhing black limb twisted about his body and pulled him into a swirling, tar-like entity obscuring the outside of my window.

How this had come to be, how this creature of darkness had my child, how Evander had managed to escape just enough to reach out to me—I would never know. But my son, I knew, was determined and whip smart. He had found a way. And I would not let it be in vain. I would not let him slip through my fingers again.

"Evander. Evander, baby, I'm coming. Evander, I'm coming." I repeated these words like a mantra as I dragged the half-demolished toilet seat over to the window and climbed atop it. It rocked on its uneven footing beneath my weight, but I gripped the ledge of the window and heaved myself onto it. Glass shards embedded in the palms of my hands, blood streaming down my wrists from a dozen cuts. I could hardly tell. I reached one ragged hand out the open window toward my son as his body flailed against the blackness dragging him in, as he continued to scream my name.

I heard, muffled as if through water, the sound of Joe's voice calling from below.

"Mariam! What are you doing? Mariam, go back inside. It's not safe. Go back!"

I looked down but could only see blackness and Evander, only his face and hands reaching, screaming for me, the rest consumed by whatever had a hold of him. Was this some hole in reality that Joe could not see, just as I could not see Joe? Perhaps Evander could only appear to me. But I could not deny his existence before me now any more than I could deny my own breath.

More voices, one amplified through a megaphone, deep and authoritative, "Ma'am, please back away from the ledge."

But my child's scream mattered more.

"Evander! Evander!" I had to get to him. I had to. I reached my body further out the window, scrambling both feet onto the ledge. Still too far. I could now only see a single hand, grasping for his mother, could only hear his ever more desperate cries drowned out by the pool of black before me. The yells of Joe, of the others with him below, intensified, but I paid them no mind.

I would not lose my child twice. Never.

"I'm coming, baby," I whispered the words one last time, and leapt from the window into the void.

Avid adventurer, Anna has lived in eight countries around the world and trekked across six continents. After gaining her degree in International Relations from UBC, she moved to Squamish to rock climb and write down the complex cultural fantasy worlds that had infiltrated her brain. She's had several SF/F pieces published by Havok Publishing and an urban fantasy short story in the Retelling Her World anthology by Smash-Bear Publishing.

On Shifting Sands
by Anna Hill

Their eyes held each other's in an unwavering, untrusting stare. The ghostly glow of the sole spark lamp resting in the sand between them produced just enough light to illuminate the red of his iris', and the yellow of hers. In their youth, when the world was whole, these colors had meant nothing. Now that the world was torn, they were the mark of an enemy.

"Of all the souls I thought might wander out of the black desert and into my lamplight, I'll admit, I could never have guessed it would be you." The ghost of a grin pulled at the edges of his tightened lips.

She would never admit it aloud, but she'd been shaken to her core the moment she'd recognized the face floating in the glow as she'd approached the lamp.

She'd been stumbling through the sands for nearly five hours, thirsty, hungry, broken—both outside and in. When she'd seen the flickering light within the never-ending sea of darkness, she'd marched up the dune toward it, ignoring the possibility of finding an enemy awaiting her.

Someone else had survived. Someone else still lived.

The great battle had been a slaughter. A sea of corpses left to wither underneath the unforgiving sun, to be picked apart by ravenous vultures until all that remained were their dried bones and desecrated dreams.

The lifeless faces of the fallen flashed through her mind, the bloody bodies belonging to old and young, poor and wealthy, male and female, as many sightless red eyes as yellow.

And yet, of course, Ciarán had escaped death. When they were young and stealing bread from the marketplace, he'd always managed to escape. Only she had felt the harsh bite of the Marshal's punishing whip.

Adira rolled her shoulders, the skin tight where brutal scars marred her flesh all these years later.

"I could have killed you."

"Or I you," she returned quickly. Her fingers tensed where they rested on the grip of her sheathed sword. She could see the outline of Ciarán's right hand resting ready on the hilt of his blade.

"So why didn't you?"

"I still could."

Ciarán shook his head, no longer bothering to hold back his grin. "You haven't changed Adira. I'm glad of it." His red eyes scanned her face. "All these years and you look so much like I remember you."

The light flickered over his square jaw, his hooked nose, his too sharp cheekbones. "You look older," she spoke honestly. He was no longer the slightly plump boy from their youth. He was a man. A killer. Like herself.

Ciarán sighed, sorrow washing over his thinned features. "I feel the years like grave weights on my shoulders.

I suppose a never-ending war has a way of doing that to you."

Knowing silence fell between them, only the soft whisper of a gentle breeze shifting the endless sands surrounding them.

"You wear white." His voice snapped Adira's drifting attention back to her companion. On instinct, her grip tightened on her weapon, but she faltered when she noticed Ciarán had dropped hold of his own. His tanned hands were now folded over his crossed legs, almost as if he were praying. "That means you're a ranking officer, doesn't it."

Adira glanced down at her uniform. The once pristine fabric of her white tunic and braies pants was now heavily blemished by splotches of dried blood that appeared black in the dim lighting. Some of it was hers. Most of it was her enemies'.

"I was one." She returned her fierce gaze to Ciarán. "Now my division's blood soaks the sand."

"Along with many others." Ciarán brought his clasped hands up before his brow, touching them lightly to his forehead as he muttered softly to himself.

God's will. She couldn't hear the words, but she knew they were what he said. As she had so many times throughout her life. But not today. Not since the battle. She refused to believe so much wasted life was God's true will.

"It's quite the story," he continued. "An orphan street urchin becomes one of your Prince's chosen."

"My King's," she corrected him.

"I guess he would call himself that, wouldn't he. As does mine. That's why we find ourselves here, isn't it? Abandoned in the unforgiving desert, covered in blood. All so one brother can wear a bigger crown than the other."

Adira clenched her teeth together, flexing the muscles in her jaw. His words sounded like treason, against not only his Prince, but her King. Words like these were enough to earn the separation of his head from his body.

"Still," he moved on, ignoring her unease, "it must feel good to have risen so far in station. You did always have a way of getting people to follow you, even when your schemes were more senseless than effective. I too fell victim to your charisma. I have the scars to prove it."

"What scars?" she bit harshly at the words. "You were never caught."

"I might have outrun the Marshal, but not my father." A flash of agitation tightened Ciarán's angular face.

Adira recalled his father, or more so the pungent stench of stale alcohol that had been ever-present on the man.

"That was a long time ago." She shook her head. "Much has changed since then."

"Everything has changed since then." Ciarán laughed, though there was no humor in it. "I think some times about Great King Huran. Would he have married a woman from each bloodline if he'd known all the death his act would bring?"

"His act united our clans."

"For a brief time…and then it broke our land and its people."

Adira did not feel comfortable with where this talk was going. She had dedicated her life to her King's cause. She'd poured enough blood onto the sand to make the great river run red. She'd slain men, women, and those too young to be considered either. She couldn't allow herself to second guess her cause, or the weight of all that death would suffocate her.

"It was brave of you to light a spark lamp." She changed the subject, the small hairs on her back still bristling. "Were you not worried you might be inviting death?"

"If God's will had been for me to die, I would be back there, twisted up amongst the field of mutilated corpses. No, it's not yet my time for death." There was an unmistakable sadness in Ciarán's voice, as if he almost wished to be proven wrong.

God must have a wicked sense of humor.

The dark shadow fell over them before either had the chance to draw their weapons. Adira's body went rigid as the sharpened steel bit at her throat where the cold blade pressed ruthlessly against her skin. She watched the spark lamp's soft light dancing along the polished surface, waiting for the cruel edge to steal her last breath. When the final slice did not come, she shifted her gaze along the blade, up the black-clothed arm, to the silver mask that hovered over them.

She recognized the wickedly carved face. Metal lips were peeled back in an engraved snarl to reveal elongated, sharpened fangs for teeth. Above the flared nostrils, were bottomless black holes where the wearer's eyes should have shown through the mask. A Death's Shadow. One of her King's assassins.

Once her yellow gaze fell upon the black holed eyes, the sword fell from her neck. But the one in its right hand, the one pressed against Ciarán's throat, pushed harder against his skin.

"You sit with the enemy," the gravelly voice accused from within the disturbing mask as the assassin shifted its attention from Adira to Ciarán.

"I do," Adira responded. There was no point in creating a false narrative. It would only incite the Death Shadow's wrath. The assassins were known for their blood thirst. Just because her eyes matched the pair hidden behind the black, didn't mean she was free from the Shadow's fury.

"Have you forgotten the commands of your King?" The Shadow snarled as it leaned threateningly close to Ciarán.

Adira watched the man she'd known in her youth, waiting for terror to fill him, but his lean face remained impassive, his stern gaze never wavering from the fearsome assassin. Brave. Or senseless. She wasn't sure. But she was impressed. There were few who could face a Death Shadow without fear. She was not among them.

"I know your kind," Ciarán spoke, causing the blade pressed against his throat to slice through the first layer of skin. A small line of blood slipped along his sharp Adam's apple. "You fought like demons on the battlefield. But you are not one. You bleed and you die just as humans. My sword made sure of it."

A throaty growl curled out from behind the mask. "I will slit your throat, Red Eyes. I will send you to hell where the rest of your worthless kind rot, awaiting the death of your counterfeit King."

"If it's God's will," Ciarán whispered into the still night, leaning his head back to present his neck fully to the Shadow's blade.

Adira moved before she'd even realized her own resolve. In a single breath, her right hand snatched within the folds of her tunic, grasped the chilled metal hilt of her curved dagger, and with a swift lunge, she'd buried the entire length of the blade between the Shadow's ribs.

The weapon fell from Ciarán's neck. Three stumbling steps backwards and the silver mask flashed one final time in the lamplight, before it was swallowed by the black desert. A hissing sound slithered around them as gravity gently drug the body down the steep dune.

Adira stared in shock at her empty hand. The Shadow's corpse had stolen the dagger, leaving behind only a splattering of warm blood across her fingertips.

"Why?"

Adira's wide eyes darted toward Ciarán. His red iris' glistened in the glow of the lamp where he'd remained seated, cross-legged in the sand.

"Why?" he repeated, his voice calm, but firm.

Adira searched Ciarán's grim face, allowing the silence to stretch between them as her wild pulse thrummed through her body. She didn't have an answer. She didn't know why.

"I am your enemy." Ciarán waved a hand somberly toward Adira's front. "Just as the ones were whose blood decorates your uniform."

"I won't apologize for those I've killed in combat!" Adira asserted fiercely. She brought her bloodstained hand to her chest and wiped it along the front of her once white tunic, the Shadow's blood blending in with the rest. "I fought for my King and for my clan. As did the ones with your eyes."

"As did I." Ciarán bowed his head. "May the darkness of the desert swallow our sins." Keeping his chin low, he lifted his penetrating red gaze to meet hers once more.

Adira held his stare. "And the light reveal a landscape of fresh sands," she completed the proverb.

"Where will you go now?"

"By the stars, I'm no more than a day's journey to Ahlryth. It's held by my clan." Adira took a step away from the lamp. Its flickering flame no longer inviting.

"So, you to your clan, and me, once more, to mine." Ciarán inhaled deeply, sighing the heavy breath through his hooked nose. "Tonight, I am grateful for the past. I believe it was God's will for us to see each other again."

Adira didn't answer, for she wasn't sure she felt the same.

"Good luck, old friend." Ciarán bowed his head low, touching his folded hands to his forehead. "May God's will keep you safe."

Adira clasped her hands together and brought them to her forehead, though she didn't bow. "And also you."

Before Ciarán could raise his gaze, she was gone. Her hurried steps slipped in the lose sand of the steep dune. Her unwavering yellow gaze set before her, refusing to look back.

"May the darkness of the desert swallow our sins," she hissed through clenched teeth. "All my sins."

Did You Know …

The first bookmobile in the world was launched in 1857. It was a horse-drawn wagon created to "diffuse good literature among the rural population."

-Kasia Kowalczyk on Ebook Friendly

PEACE
BY PHOENIX MENDOZA

Lorna's been my partner for three years. I like her–she's fast on a horse, good with a gun. Silver hair shorn close to her skull and the sort of crooked mouth that looks natural around a stogie. She covers my back and makes me laugh but doesn't ask questions, and that's the sort of partner you want in containment breach enforcement. Personable, but not personal. If things get too chummy, the bad guys always know.

Funny thing about Lorna is that she believes in peace. Like, doves and Christmas songs and kumbaya bullshit. She thinks this war can end. I don't. When you grow up, you'll see, she once told me, sun reflecting off the aluminum shine of her buzz cut. Reins in one hand, a cigar in the other. You'll change your mind. Soften up. I was an angry girl too, when I was your age.

I won't. Grow up, maybe, but change my mind? Nah. My family was killed in the first invasion. Cracked open like eggs and fried in the scald of the sun, their blood sizzling into pale mauve patties like they were hamburger meat and Earth was cast iron. The alien fuckers touched down in tube shaped space ships like the canisters inside an airgun, blasted the surface, leveled everything. Those of us who survived the attack inevitably lost people. Some of us lost everyone. Lorna's all alone in the shield barracks with no family just like me, so I know she has a story to tell, like I have a story to tell. We won't tell our stories, though, not even three years later. We don't need to–theylre all the same.

 She's stitched me up with fishing line, she's popped my shoulder back into the socket. I hauled her across five miles of smoking desert when her horse spooked at a shield malfunction–something in the hologram fritzed, she fell and broke her ankle and made some joke about Butch Cassidy and the Sundance Kid. We trust each other about the shit that counts, but we don't talk. Not about loss, not about our old lives dead and smoking, not about peace. Not about how one paves the way for the other in some people, obliterates it completely in others.

The gig is dangerous, but simple: ride to the edge of the defense shield's perimeter, and kill anything that tries to cross it. We're border control, essentially, for a brand new border. The enemy can take on any form to trick you–your mom, your dead husband, an innocent kid, your childhood dog. They play mind games, sing a song to get in your head like sailor's sirens. To work in containment breach you gotta have thick skin, an iron constitution. You gotta be able to put a bullet in grandma before the glamor is broken and you see her for what she really is: jellied slug with white pill pupils on eye stalks, a hundred stubby tardigrade feet. They melt in the sun, instead of fry. Lorna hates the smell so we torch them instead of leaving them at the shield perimeter to liquify like some of the newer, sloppier Enforcers. They don't weigh much dead. We throw them on a tarp and drag them to a pile, squirt some lighter fluid, toss a match and voila–bonfire at the end of a hard day, stack of sirens burning to a burnt-sugar tar while Lorna and I pass a bottle of wine.

I like white, Lorna likes red. Funny, that the girl who lives for war sips the color of surrender, and the one who believes there's an end in sight sips the color of blood.

I could ask her who she lost. Daughter, maybe, she's old enough. Husband–wife, more likely. It isn't my business but part of me wants to know who she's offing every day out there on the frontlines, knee-deep in slug slime, sawed-off cocked and ready. You spend three years working and drinking with a woman, you get curious about what ghosts she's fighting. After a 9-to-5 of ghostbusting, I think that's only human. I have a war inside me, silent, and maybe part of me wants to see if her's matches.

Last month I shot my father, my mother, my sister, my best friend. Last week it was my first grade teacher, my soccer coach, my favorite aunt. Yesterday, and the day before that, and the day before that, it was Lorna. Her silver hair glinting, her smile soft and lopsided. It fucks with my head to feel her solid, burning bulk right beside me at the same time I stare down the barrel at her pleading face, and squeeze the trigger. Wide, tear-shining eyes, plum-dark tongue in a mouth spouting those last pleas for peace before she crumples to the sand in a heap of limbs and linen. Then she transforms, the illusion shattered. No matter how many times I see it, no matter how many times I shoot knowing that's a slug in disguise, it's still so goddamned hard to do. My heart pounds, my hands shake. I'm grateful we fight back to back, so she never sees the hesitance in my traitorous trigger finger.

After a solid ten days of it, I drink too much at the bonfire. Polish off my pinot and start eying her malbec. Pretending the world didn't end, actually, and we're just two ladies at a winery. Aliens didn't come for us, what's left of humanity isn't preserved in a domed holographic shield, there's no need for folks to patrol it. No sand, no slugs, no sadness. She notices me brooding about it and pours a generous slosh into my tin camping mug without a word. I realize if the world hadn't ended and the slugs hadn't come and humanity hadn't been whittled down to survivors, the likelihood I would have ever met Lorna whittles right down to nothing, too. There's no reason for a girl like me to have met a woman like her, there's no reason for a woman like her to befriend a girl like me. No fucking reason at all for us to meet out in the wild under some grape arbor in the Sierras. We were brought together by death, by necessity. That's all.

Who did you lose? I want to ask, the words itching. But that's not what comes out: "I know you think there's a chance for reconciliation with them down the line, I know that. But I just. If I don't kill every fucking slug I can, is it even worth it? What's the goddamned point of the job, if–" I cut myself off, spill wine into the sand. She reaches out and puts a rough hand on my knee to squeeze it.

"Princess," she says, which is what she calls me. Like I have some kingdom to inherit. Like I'm locked in a fucking tower somewhere, and need rescuing. Like I'm not a slug slayer just like her. It's funny because it should be condescending, but it's not. It's sweet, like riesling, like the wild happenstance of the world as we know it going up in flames and that bringing us together. So tightly together it's her I see at the end of my barrel when the slugs look into my heart and become what I'll miss most. "You're busy looking back, and I'm looking forward. Imagining a life where we don't have to do the job. Where there isn't a perimeter to enforce. I'm thinking of a little house, and a vegetable garden out back, and a girl at my side."

I look at her like I've never seen her before. Lorna. Lips stained, shape hazy through tears and smoke, something so soft about even the hard edges she's honed. "I had a veggie garden, before the war," I tell her, and somehow it feels like a confession. "Snails ruined it."

She throws her head back and laughs like I'm a riot. I watch her, bewildered. Funny, how the old woman can look ahead at all the life left to live, and the young one is stuck in the tar-pits of the past.

Slapping my thigh gently, Lorna thumbs into the seam of my cargos. "Listen–that's how gardening goes. You plant stuff, it gets crisped in the sun when you forget to water, or a rabbit digs it up, or the goddamned slugs get it. But I think the hope–the growing part. It's worth it. Just to plant a little seed in the dirt and watch it sprout when you love on it."

 Love on it. Hits me like a blow, and so suddenly, I feel dead sober. When you grow up, you'll see, she told me once, and for the first time in a long time I allow myself to think of it again: growing from an angry girl into something else, a green shoot from a cracked seed. The shield coming down because we don't need it anymore, Lorna and I at a winery, because someone at the end of the world has learned how to grow grapes and ferment.A sunset to ride into, instead of a warzone. Chewed tomato leaves. Someone to weed with. A treaty. Peace.

Beth Sherman's writing has been published in more than 200 literary magazines, including Flash Frog, Gone Lawn, Tiny Molecules, 100 Word Story, Fictive Dream, and Bending Genres. Her work is featured in Best Microfiction 2024 and she's the winner of the Smokelong Quarterly 2024 Workshop prize. A multiple Pushcart, Best Small Fictions, and Best of the Net nominee, she can be reached on X, Bluesky or Instagram @bsherm36.

GRAVE MISDEEDS, FUNNY BONES
BY BETH SHERMAN

When Aunt Helen arrives unannounced, you are busy lacing the plum duff with arsenic. "Lor," says Auntie, "ain't you gettin' to be a fine baker." You smile, wishing she'd climb back in her pony cart and return to Yorkshire. As she chatters away, you boil the suet, gather the currents you've picked, spread a clean white sheet on the table. The ghost of your dead husband hovers near the stove, watching intently. "'Eard a new fella's courtin ya," Aunt Helen says. "Lucky lass." You offer her some spirits to curb her tongue, resist the urge to serve her the deadly pudding. "Careful, love," says your husband, his face a ghastly shade of grey, his cheeks nearly transparent. "Don't want to overegg it." You realize too late how fully he understood you, how much he appreciated your devilish ways. "A girl's gotta keep livin', auntie," you say. The wraith that was your husband guffaws and you spoon a dollop of his laugh into the dessert you'll serve to Bill.

Publishing Check List!

Think you're ready to indie publish your book? Let's find out!

1) Edit your manuscript as many times as you can (while staying sane!)

2) Find a critique partner, or beta readers to do an initial read for any major problems or improvements. If you're not sure what to ask your beta readers or critique partners, you can do a quick google search for "Questions to Ask Beta Readers" and find lots of great lists.

3) Hire an editor. Even after your own edits and the input of beta readers, you'll still miss some problems only professional editors can pick up! Whether it's for plot, character, development, grammar, or sentence structure, an editor will take your book from feeling amateurish, to being professional.

4) Learn how to format books or hire a formatter. It's very important that you take this step BEFORE getting your book's cover since designers will need to know the spine thickness.

5) Design your cover or hire a designer. You can find hundreds of amazing artists/designers on Instagram or who are talented at covers. Just search: #bookcoverdesigner

6) Research the different distribution companies. Between KDP, Ingramspark, Barnes&Noble, BookBaby, BookVault and more, you'll have plenty of options for printing and distributing your book. Do your research to see which will work best for you.

7) Upload your files and choose a release day!

8) Plan your cover reveal and pre-orders announcement on the same day to maximize sales. Don't forget to let family and friends help you reveal the cover by offering pre-made graphics!

9) Market, market, market your book all the way until release day. Don't stop talking about it!

10) Celebrate on release day! You've just published a book!

THE WEREWOLF CONUNDRUM
BY TODD SULLIVAN

I have a confession to make: I am writing a werewolf novel.

In some ways, writing a narrative centered around lycanthropy feels self-defeating. Though everyone knows what a werewolf is, very few can name a popular werewolf character. Ask anyone to name a well-known vampire, and they can rattle off Dracula, Lestat, Blade, Louis, Edward Cullen, Lilith, Moribus, Alucard, Barnabus Collins, Spike, Vampirella. The list goes on.

Vampire fiction has garnered numerous breakthrough hits, and this has inspired many writers to try their hand at the narrative. I myself have had vampire fiction published, from short stories to novellas. I have been fascinated with the mythos since I was a child, and it still remains one of my favorite narratives to write.

The werewolf, however, has had anemic success in popular culture. One or two movies may be recalled if the average person was pressed, with possibly fewer novels, and no characters. Keeping that in mind as I undertook the task of delving into the literary landscape of lycanthropy, I found myself wondering why the vampire is so much more popular than the werewolf. I know I am not alone in this query, as I have seen it posed multiple times in social media groups focused around the werewolf.

With the intention of fostering the best possible parameters to craft a novel that can produce the success of vampire fiction, I asked myself a simple question: what makes the vampire so much more compelling than the werewolf in the eyes of discerning readers and moviegoers?

Below are the reasons, as far as I can see, that explain the discrepancy in the werewolf vs. vampire debate.

One of the greatest disadvantages of werewolf narratives is that they are forced to take place in rural areas. Unlike the vampire, which is supernatural and often depicted as having various powers at their fingertips, the lycanthrope is preternatural and more pure in its defining characteristics. The rule of the werewolf is simple: at the full moon, a human transforms into a human/wolf hybrid. The werewolf cannot become mist, cannot fly as a bat, scale walls like a lizard, lift cars with their bare hands or leap down great heights to land catlike on their feet. Often times, the werewolf, in its human form, is no more powerful than a regular person.

The werewolf, essentially, is a human that has been cursed wild, and in the wild it must exist if it does not want to be hunted and killed. Unlike the vampire, which has various ways in which it can be killed, the method to kill a werewolf is far more simple: a silver bullet striking a vital organ. This weakness is a serious Achilles heel, especially today. One thing modern civilization has is plenty of bullets and plenty of silver.

Most werewolf narratives place the lycanthrope in a rural setting. John Landis' American Werewolf in London (1981) begins with two backpackers hiking through the moors of Yorkshire, England, when a werewolf attacks them. One of the backpackers is killed, but the other is saved by the villagers after being bitten by the beast. How do the villagers save him? With something as simple as guns, and in the case of this narrative universe, silver is not even necessary to get the job done.

The original werewolf in the John Landis' movie had been living in the moors for at least a generation, and as soon as an urban element is introduced to its rural world, the beast is hunted down and killed. When the bitten backpacker, now cursed with lycanthropy, returns to London, he transforms at the next full moon, goes on a rampage, is cornered in an alley by the police, and is killed in a hail of bullets in less than twenty-four hours after he first succumbs to the curse.

Place a werewolf in any urban location on the planet in this modern world and the result will invariably be the same. Even in small town settings, such as Stephen King's Cycle of the Wolf, the werewolf only manages to live several months before it is eventually killed by a young 10-year-old boy in a wheelchair.

A werewolf attempting to live in any highly or mildly populated area suffers unique problems that vampires do not have. A vampire is at home amongst the humans who provide it sustenance. Vampires are cool, calculating, and intelligent. It is hard to imagine one being killed by a child in a wheelchair. The vampire's violence exists in the shadows, away from the prying eyes of mankind. They are meticulous, stalking their prey before striking with lethal force.

A werewolf, on the other hand, is generally conveyed as a rabid dog attacking whatever comes across its path. In American Werewolf in London, the cursed backpacker falls in love with a young nurse who spends the entire movie trying to help him. Yet at the end of the film, when he transforms into the wolf and she tries to reason with him, he lunges at her and is killed by the aforementioned policemen's bullets.

A werewolf cannot live in the city, for the full moon is its greatest strength and its greatest weakness. It loses control once a month, transforming into the beast. However, placing the lycanthrope in unpopulated settings makes it more difficult for readers and audiences to connect with the character. In America, for instance, 80% of the population lives in urban areas. Around the world, 55% of the human population lives in cities. Readers are used to concrete highways, shopping malls, fancy restaurants, public transportation, trendy bars, relaxing parks, chic nightclubs. They are not used to vast forested expanses and majestic mountains, the only places a werewolf could survive for any length of time.

Readers are going to connect more readily with the well-dressed, sophisticated vampire stalking the city streets. They will find it more difficult to submerge within the point of view of the human wearing flannel shirts and corduroy pants, living in a cabin in the moors and fearing the next full moon which brings about the ensuring transformation that will have it go on a murderous killing spree which will, in most reasonably populated areas, end in its eventual execution.

This leads to the second reason vampires enjoy more popularity than werewolves. Vampires are historically seen as rich nobleman or lords of their domain. Dracula, the titular character in Bran Stoker's novel, is a Count in Transylvania who lives in a high castle above those who serve him. A derivative of this classic figure is Strahd von Zarvoich, a major villain from the Dungeons & Dragons campaign Ravenloft. Like Dracula, he is master of Barovia, a forested land surrounded by mist. He is singularly powerful and extraordinary wealthy. When his authority is questioned in Christine Golden's Vampire of the Mists, he proclaims, "I am Barovia!" In his realm, all must bow down to him alone.

Whether people will actually admit this or not, the idea of being unquestionably served is a strong desire humans hold. We want to be masters, our whims made manifest by our servants. And within vampire narratives, where do we often find the wolf? In both Dracula and Vampire of the Mists, the wolves are reduced to guard dogs for their undead masters. They prowl the gates of castles, they protect vampire lords sleeping the day away in their crypts. In Vampire of the Mists, when a werewolf enters the story, she is merely a plaything of Strahd, and quakes and flees with her tail between her legs at his fiery temper.

In Len Wiseman's Underworld (2003), we once again see vampires living in opulence. They lounge in mansions, drive luxury cars, and move with impunity in the human world. Vampires are the elite, the 1% of the one percent, whereas the Lycans (the werewolves) live in sewers and subway tunnels. Lycans dress in plain clothes, when clothed at all. Our first view of them in Underworld have two werewolves fighting each other for sport while others stand around cheering the savagery of the match. Their leader, Lucian, after stopping the fight, scolds them by saying, "You're acting like a pack of rabid dogs!"

A similar dynamic between the vampire, which is depicted as belonging to the upper crusts of society, and the much more modest werewolf living in a small house, is seen in Stephenie Meyer's Twilight. The Cullen family, the vampires of the novel, are fantastically rich. They own mansions that cost millions, dress in designer clothes, and own rare and expensive cars. The werewolf characters, on the other hand, live on a reservation. Reservations abound with poverty, which is statistically double that of the rest of America. While the vampire increases his personal wealth through trading stocks, the werewolf, when in human form, is depicted in the movie version of Twilight as being a mechanic who can detail the engine of a truck.

When seeing how these these two characters are drawn, one can easily answer the question of which one readers and audiences prefer to imagine themselves as: vampires that have billions at their disposal, or werewolf laborers who get dirty doing manual work?

Finally, within the vampire mythology, the vampire usually has a more desirable existence than the werwolf does in the lycanthrope mythology. In Anthony Waller's American Werewolf in Paris (1998), the backpacker is attacked by a werewolf in a rave, survives, and becomes a werewolf at the next full moon, where he murders multiple innocent people. In John Fawcett's Gingersnaps (2000), the teen girl is bitten by what's believed to be a dog, is infected with lycanthropy and is eventually killed by her little sister. In Joe Dante's Howling (1981), the reporter barely survives a werewolf attack and is killed when she transforms into a werewolf on the nightly news; in Mike Nichols' Wolf (1994), the businessman is bitten by a wolf and begins the slow transformation into a full wolf, never able to return back to human form. In Joe Johnston's The Wolfman (2010), the main character is bitten by a werewolf that turns out to be his father and is eventually killed by the woman he loves.

Two noticeable storylines reveal themselves in werewolf narratives. Most of them end with the werewolf dying a violent death. There are exceptions, but the demise of the werewolf is generally associated with the literature. Audiences are not meant to be seduced by the power of the lycanthrope. They are meant to fear the transformation, to see it as a tragic outcome of a gruesome encounter, and to search for ways to cure the curse.

Which leads to the second aspect of the werewolf mythology. The curse of lycanthropy is not offered to the character, it is forced upon them. Contrast this to vampirism, which is considered a dark gift. In most vampire lore, a human is drained of blood and then asked if they want to drink the blood of the vampire in order to join them in undeath.

Lycanthropy is similar to rape, whereas vampirism requires consent.

In most vampire narratives, the vampire does not meet a violent death. Here, too, there are some exceptions. Dracula is stabbed through the heart with a wooden stake and decapitated, though the legend of Dracula is as prevalent today as when the novel first came out in 1897, and derivatives of the character are numerous in popular culture.

The vampire's death is a minority in vampire literature, not the rule. Most narratives have vampires living on after the last page has been read, or as the credits roll. Conversely, the werewolf's death is the norm, not the exception. The werewolf is simply considered a beast that needs to put down, whereas the vampire is considered a human that has transcended into something better than it was before.

Despite these many disadvantages of the lycanthrope narrative, I am writing a werewolf novel. Ultimately, there is something noble in the mythology. It is a challenge to any writer who decides to undertake the journey into the wild. Lycanthropes are of the natural world, and in this day in age when the planet is threatened by so many artificial pollutants pumped into the waters and atmosphere, maybe it is time we remember that, like the werewolf, nature is wild, majestic, deadly, yet also surprisingly vulnerable. The tragedy of the werewolf narrative perfectly reflects the dangers of modernization consuming the natural world around it. And though this concept may not be as popular as the vampire narrative, it is still a story worth telling, if only as a cautionary tale.

Words From the Heart

SHE WROTE LIKE BURROUGHS

BY JAMES TUCKER

Everyone is writing like Burroughs,
Trying to be like Burroughs.
Trying to resurrect Burroughs.

(In his grave he spins.)

My wife wrote like Burroughs.
Toed the line, walked the walk.
Danced that dance, necromanced.
We fucked in bug crawling romance.
She wrote like Burroughs.
She died like Burroughs.

James Tucker is a writer from Charleston, SC. His works have appeared in Adelaide magazine, Tall Tale TV, MetaStellar Magazine and others. He is featured in the upcoming anthology: Universe of Attractions, from Dead Fish Publishing.

MEDICATION TIME

BY D.F WESTON

a sharp chirp, a whistle
a tilt in the throat, a dote
on each small blue one
a tiny touch, almost slip
fine as whisps, horse tips
shakes there, then gone
like salty sips of sea water
my mind comes back after
backing away from splashes
of slicing grains, my wounds
sterilised, but the pain remains
muted under soothing stains
of royal red and greying green
it's like that, only afterwards
a laugh

D.F Weston is a UK based writer featured in online magazines and has released spoken word albums online.

Through Your Eyes, I See

By Ceci Li

Through your eyes,
I see the colors of the rainbow.
Red in the roses.
Blue in the sky.
Green in the grass.
Yellow in the stars

Through your eyes,
I see hope for the future.
The aspiration of a dream.
The desire for living.
The yearning for nature.
The wish for tomorrow.

Through your eyes,
I see love for humanity.
Compassion for the diligent.
Empathy for the poor.
Cherishing for the young and old
Devotion for me.

Through your eyes,
I see the world in its presence.
Blooming flowers in the spring.
Fluttering fireflies in the summer,
Breathtaking foliage in the fall.
Evanescent snowflake in the winter.

Through your eyes,
My loneliness vanished.
I forgave God for shutting the blinds in my sight,
With your guidance, a new window opened.

Through your eyes,
I see the light shining through my darkness.
The world was unreachable before I became we,
But now, it's at my fingertips.

Writer bio: Ceci is an aspiring YA contemporary writer, an essential healthcare worker, a cat-less cat lady, and a human with a cringy sense of humor according to her two children.

THIS HEAVY HEART

REMOVE THE MOON

BY AMELIA CLAWFORD

This heart in my chest is heavy,
but perhaps that is not all such a bad thing.
Heavy just means full:

Full of sorrows like rocks that bruise my ribs,
yes;
full of regrets like pebbles stuck in every crack,
yes;
but full of joys, too,
poured in between and all around the rocks
and the pebbles
like sand from the sea
or soil from a garden
weighing down this heavy heart,
keeping it
full.

Remove the moon, and set the tide free
Let all the sea's children ride free

I know you think it absurd,
to let the waters far and wide free

But haven't you wanted to
see the other side free?

All of those times you
took my hand and cried, "Free

The forests and the birds," well,
now they've all died free

So remove the moon,
and set the tide free.

Amelia E. Clawford has been writing for about ten years—or maybe five? Seven? Whatever. She's a writer, not a mathematician. Anyway, she has spent those years becoming weirder and more erratic, so take that how you will. Questionable normalcy aside, she hopes that her writing glorifies God and edifies her readers.

Moon Eats the World

by D.F. Weston

Last night, sleepers slept
as Moon's jaws were awide
sunken eyes to the skies.

Stars hymning, humming
howling at the wildly wonderful
heaven who they harboured faith.

She starved away, stomach growling
like wolves in dead of woods
without a look, she saw us at foot.

Moon couldn't resist, with a chomp
here, a munch there, a nibble at edges
savouring all spices, all herbs, all hedges.

Then it disappeared in a second
though not full, but satiated
she wandered off alone and meditated.

D.F Weston is a UK based writer featured in online magazines and has released spoken word albums online.

Lost Between Our Midnights

by Meisha Jean

Tender is the night for a broken heart
Bluer is the scar on the collarbone
A starstruck in vain, a singer revenged
Midnight, she cries and you're sleeping, shut off.

Bygone Eighties mirrored in your wet eyes
So far so fragile, falling out of grasp
Falling into pieces, Heart collapses
At your voice, pierced through and through, disgrace.

Oxytocin lacking, on command is
Serotonin, before bed sky turns green
The color of your old washed sweater.

Dawn is sour, not orange. Someday it will
Smell like your perfume. A glance through this hope
Bluer, sadder, someday, it will taste like… dawn is tender.

Tender is the night for a wistful heart
Greener is the scar on the collarbone
A starstruck in mind, a singer appeased
Midnight, she dreams and you're far gone, a ghost.

Meisha Jean is a young fashion design student and self-published author in France who thrives in creation, whatever the medium is. She started writing poetry at fifteen years old, after her literature teacher introduced her to poet Charles Baudelaire. She enjoys exploring her own emotions and life experience through her designs and writings, inspired by literary works, surrealism, Chinese poetry and art, and music (alternative pop, classical, soft rock). Melancholy, theatrical atmosphere and raw emotion may summarize her art style.

Interviews with Fellow Writers Passing on their Advice!

MERGING COZY & HORROR WITH
A.L. DAVIDSON & NATHANIEL LUSCOMBE

AL Davidson (she/they/he) walks the line between horror and cozy perfectly. They write an insane amount of words a year, and have released a handful of novels and novellas independently and through small publishers. Among her titles are The Scientist, the Spaceman, and the Stars Between Them, When the Rain Begins to Burn, The Night Farm, and Lover, Thy Name is Pestilence. Never one to shy away from the uncomfortable, you can always expect their books to shock you in some way.

I'm Nathaniel Luscombe, and thank you for joining us for today's interview, A.L. Davidson! We're very excited to dive into what your writing means to you and why you do it.

Q. To begin, what fuels your writing?

A. Hi! Thank you for having me! Without overcomplicating it, a deep rooted love of storytelling is about 75% of the cocktail of things that fuels my writing. It was somewhat inevitable that this was the path I'd choose for myself. Growing up in the '90s and 2000s during the height of Disney animation and the sweeping wave of JRPGs and anime, I'd gained a heavy love for lore, world building, and expansive stories that never left me.

When other kids were outside playing, I was inside making my own manga or losing hours on the family computer on Storybook Weaver making up my own books. It's that classic I always dreamed of being a writer thing most of us suffer from. It's my biggest passion, joy, and reason for living. Writing is who I am at my core, and I feel really weird when I'm not at the keyboard. The other 25% is a mixture of auDHD and spite, so that probably doesn't help!

Q. It's always amazing to see such deep-rooted love for storytelling inside of an author. Are there themes or ideas that you work hard to incorporate within your writing? If so, why are they important to you?

A. Yes! I actually list them in my bio because I tend to repeat the same core themes throughout. I always say I "tell stories about ghosts, grief, isolation, queerness, ecohorror, life with disabilities, space exploration, and the human condition." For me, a focus on human-centered storytelling is key to every story I do, whether I'm in the cozy corner or the hole of horrifying heartbreak - the two places I tend to spend most of my time. Telling stories about authentic, flawed, people in authentic, flawed relationships is at the core of everything I do no matter what genre I'm dabbling in.

Q. That's incredible. Are there certain themes you find easier to write in cozy vs horror and vice versa?

A. I think if I did normal horror, I'd probably have more struggles going back and forth, but since I have really human-focused stories that are all rooted in romance and relationships, the jump between genres isn't too difficult for me and a lot of the themes I tend to gravitate toward often overlap. One of my favorite writing tools is an amazing little book called Thinking Like A Romance Writer by Dahlia Evans, which is a phrase book of terminology for sensual writing - and I use it more for my horror than anything!

There's such a thin line between the two, which is why horrormance works so well (in my humble opinion), and why every craft store has spooky-cute decor the moment summer rolls around. I've been told on numerous occasions that my horror is cozy, that it feels like a warm, terrifying hug. I do find that the character building aspects come easier in the cozies, because I have time to build and let the characters breathe, while in horror things are actively trying to kill them so they have to develop on the fly, or have to be written in a way that they already feel developed in a believable manner since the focus shifts so drastically.

Q. Fascinating. That answer is both unexpected and expected. Cozy horror is such a vibe, and something we need more of. What better time for a hug than during all the terrifying moments. Are you writing what you always intended to write, or has there been some self-discovery and an acceptance of change along the way?

A. I'm definitely not writing what I intended to write - I started in YA fantasy with fairies and royal hierarchies! - but I think I'm writing what I was always meant to write. My first published book was a YA fantasy written in middle school, and even back then I was more focused on my two male characters and their relationship than the literal love interest and main romance. My teenage writing was filled with stories about nature, the horrors of capitalism, found family, and the essence of scifi - with cozy vibes and horror elements, of course. So while the genres have changed, as have I, I think that the foundation of what became my niche was always there. I'm now no longer afraid to make my characters queer, or lean into the horror and more intense elements, but looking back at some of those old stories you can really see that the things I love to write about haven't shifted much. They've mostly just become more authentic.

Q. Which of your books would you recommend a reader start with?

A. Since I write a variety of genres, it depends on what you enjoy! The easiest answer would be The Night Farm, since it's not only my most popular series but the most accessible and approachable. The cozy Stardew Valley vibes and the spooky but cute aesthetic really vibes with a lot of readers. But if you're looking for something that will get under your skin, I recommend one of my horrormances like All For The Blood of The Lamb or Lover, Thy Name is Pestilence. The nice thing about horror, and my library of books, is that I dip into a variety of subgenres so there's a little something for everyone in there!

Thank you for taking time to do this interview. You heard it from him first. Be sure to grab one of their titles ASAP and dive into a wonderful and terrifying world unlike anything you've read before.

KENNEDY COLE BIO: Kennedy Cole is a speculative author born and raised in North Carolina. A graduate of UNC Wilmington, Kennedy lives by the beach with her partner and enjoys playing games, puzzling, sipping matcha, and collecting tattoos. Her debut horror novel, THERE USED TO BE PEOPLE HERE, will be published with Berkley at Penguin Random House in November 2026. You can find more info about her at kennedyreadsandwrites.com, or on Instagram @kennedyreadsandwrites.

I am Anna Ford, and I sat down with author Kennedy Cole to chat about her upcoming debut THERE USED TO BE PEOPLE HERE and her writing journey.

Q. Congratulations on your debut novel, There Used to Be People Here! When did you first know that Samuel's story was one you wanted to tell?

A. Thank you so much! Honestly, it was when I first began writing the story. I dove into THERE USED TO BE PEOPLE HERE as a way to fill time after my mentor asked to read a novel I'd been querying previously, to no success. My novel began as a continuation of a short story I'd written the semester before, about an interaction between a young man experiencing his first night at a gay bar and an ominously strange older gentleman. Chapter one began with the aftermath of the short story, originally titled "Danny in the Bathroom," and a murder investigation led by who's now one of my dearest characters, Samuel Barkley.

Samuel being the only Black detective in Wenton, Mississippi's police department was a decision I made shortly after beginning THERE USED TO BE PEOPLE HERE. As a Black writer, this is the first novel I've written where my main character also matched my skin tone. I've heard other writers of color speak on this before, but it really is normalized among our communities to assume a character is white before anything else. It's not something I was directly taught, but it is something I inadvertently taught myself by consuming, and honestly prioritizing, books with all white casts and stories that ignored racial identities.

Samuel's story began as a way to process my own. His is one of discovering self-identity, overcoming hatred for his own existence, and learning to love who he is despite how everyone else sees him. Mine isn't exactly quite as dark and dreadful, but it is similar in that Samuel's experience as the only Black detective matches many of my own. I've been the only Black girl at my school, all the way from K-12. I've been the only Black girl in a city's entire downtown district. I've been the only Black person in a church.

Samuel's story challenged me to analyze how I've felt as the only one in a room full of people who don't look like me. Yes, it was very challenging. But it was also enlightening, fulfilling, and overall lovely. I wouldn't change his story one bit.

Q. You once posted on Instagram that you wrote your first story in the fifth grade. How has your journey as a writer changed since that first project, and what about your writing has remained constant?

A. When I first started writing in fifth grade, I had no idea what I was doing. I'd recently read a published book written by a sixth grader, and felt inspired by the notion that I—a child—could also create worlds and characters and share them with other people, without needing to be a full adult. The first "book" I wrote was a thirty-two page adventure about my beta fish, Charlie. Not only were all of the other characters named after my classmates, but the adventure itself mimicked a similar model to another popular fish's journey: Nemo.

Needless to say, the first story I ever wrote as a fifth grader who swore she'd be an author one day was pretty childish, and overall, shamelessly self-indulgent. What I did learn, though, is that I could write very quickly. Since then, there hasn't been a time in my life when I wasn't actively writing, editing, revising, or considering a new novel idea to hyper-fixate on for the next few years. I ended high school with several books written, all of which I worked on during class instead of paying attention or at the family computer once I'd finished my homework.

Since my first project, I can easily say I've become a lot more purposeful about the stories I tell. I'm not writing about the first thing that comes to mind anymore, or naming my characters after people I've barely spoken to. After all this time, though, my self-indulgence remains. I write what I love because I love it, which is how I think all writing should start. My writing is also often indirectly infused with my own personal experiences, be it a random memory my characters can't forget, a lasting grudge they hold, or the way they view the world. It's like my way of processing what's going on around me through eyes that belong to me, but aren't my own.

My writing, too, is still quick. I've learned how to write a lot of words in a short span of time, which is extremely useful when it comes to my writing process. The only frustrating part is the period between projects, when I have to decide what comes next.

Q. What was it like to write and query your first novel while pursuing your undergraduate degree?

A. Terrifying, to say the least. As a disclaimer, I've always written outside of class. I think it's a good exercise to challenge yourself as a writer to have personal projects away from assignments, not only because it offers an escape from the rigorous educational landscape, but also because writing outside of the classroom helps to prevent it from feeling like "work."

All that to say, writing AND querying was a new challenge I faced head on while also maintaining my college credit hours, and it was definitely a lot to process. I finished writing THERE USED TO BE PEOPLE HERE during the summer, but most of my revisions took place at the start of my Spring semester after a group of my friends/beta readers returned their feedback. Working on novel revisions on top of class assignments—I was taking a novel writing class, an introduction to publishing class, and a book building class all simultaneously—took discipline, dedication, and determination. TLDR: I locked in.

I'm extremely grateful for the help and support from my professors, who helped me prepare my querying materials prior to sending out my first batch. I'm also thankful for the people who believed in me and encouraged me during the querying process. As a student, it's really easy to not be taken seriously when you say you're going to query the novel you wrote while learning as an undergraduate in a creative writing program. Without the encouragement of my friends, peers, and professors, I would've had a harder time with continuing to query while attending school. In a strange way, it was also helpful to have work to focus on once I sent out my first queries. They were a nice distraction from the void of agents who I constantly feared were either planning to reject me, or actively ghosting me.

Q. There Used to Be People Here focuses on race and queerness in the South. What was your favorite part of writing Samuel and Harvey's story? What was exploring these themes like in conjunction with the speculative nature of the book?

A. What an impossible question! Samuel and Harvey both complement each other in ways that I think make them perfect partners, both in and out of the Wenton Police Department. Throughout the story, Samuel consistently struggles with the idea of wanting to be "invisible," which I think many POC—including myself—have considered at a certain point. To be specific, it's difficult for Samuel to accept his identity in a place where he feels pressured to (and basically does) represent the entire Black community. Harvey's struggle is similar to Samuel's in that he's also ashamed of his identity as a gay man, yet at the same time, Harvey is much more aware of his romantic desires than Samuel is. Throw in the fact that Harvey loathes his job, and the two of them have a lot of angst and tension to unload over the course of their weeklong murder investigation/horrifying odyssey.

My favorite part of writing about Samuel and Harvey wasn't a singular moment, but the way these smaller, more thematic moments unfolded on the page. THERE USED TO BE PEOPLE HERE is a horror story, first and foremost, but it's also the chronicle of a Black man learning to love who he is, as he is. It's the tale of an artist rekindling his love for painting and breaking free from the "stable job" his father imposed on him. It's the story of two gay men finding each other in a room that would prefer them apart.

My novel's speculative story elements are well intertwined with Samuel's desire to be "invisible," and Harvey's hope of living in a world where queer communities aren't pushed to the outskirts of town. In fact, THERE USED TO BE PEOPLE HERE's primary antagonist—parasitic aliens known as taur—tempt Harvey and Samuel with this very idea: the beguiling concept of oneness. I won't divulge too much of the plot, but there are multiple moments where Samuel seriously considers what this world would look like, even if it means letting the taur win. Harvey's balance to Samuel's internal torment is definitely one of the best parts of this story, in my opinion.

Q. How has working on your second book differed from There Used to Be People Here?

A. My second book—whose title I currently cannot divulge—has definitely been a much different beast to tackle. For one, it's dual POV and follows the relationship between a modern-day mother and son, rather than two police detectives in 1970s Mississippi. While I do think Samuel and Harvey both play pivotal main character roles in THERE USED TO BE PEOPLE HERE, I wouldn't change my choice to keep the story only in Samuel's third-person POV. Balancing two different voices, character arcs, and plot lines, while ALSO having them intertwine over the course of a mysterious new storyline, has been nothing short of exhilarating, to say the least.

Another key difference is my second novel's pace and tone. THERE USED TO BE PEOPLE HERE is a quickly paced mystery/thriller that unfolds over the course of seven days. In contrast, my second book has a much longer timeline that, as of now, I'm not sure how much time will take, but I do know it will be much longer than a week. Figuring out how to balance the pacing with my character's development, decisions, and emotions is something I'm not really used to, if I'm being honest. Breaking out of the habit of pushing scenes and events close together and using time skips comfortably has been one of my biggest challenges so far.

As I write this, I'm a fourth of the way through and excited to keep writing. And of course, I'm even more excited to share it with you one day!

Q. What do you hope people take away from reading There Used to Be People Here?

A. This question is extremely important to me, and I'm really grateful to be able to answer it here for the first time, ahead of what I'm sure will be many others. Out of all the things I explore in THERE USED TO BE PEOPLE HERE, what resonates most with me as its writer is Samuel's character arc. Samuel starts as a Black man in an America that hates him, and though this doesn't technically change by the end of the story, what does is the way that Samuel views himself and his value. One of the first lines I wrote at the beginning of my novel is Samuel's inner dialogue describing himself as "worth nothing at all." By the end, Samuel has not only accepted that he is worthy of being loved, but also realized that his virtue doesn't hinge on where he lives and what he does, but who he is as a human being.

What I hope that readers take away from reading THERE USED TO BE PEOPLE HERE is this: that the perceptions of others—especially the perceptions perpetuated by the country we live in—do not define them. We live in a world where we're taught to conform, to blend in, to be quiet and sit down and pay attention, or else we'll fall behind. This is not only dangerous, but simply untrue. My hope is that readers leave feeling inspired and seen, not just queer folk or people of color, but anyone who's been alone in a room and felt they weren't worthy of being there. You matter, and you're exactly who I'm writing for.

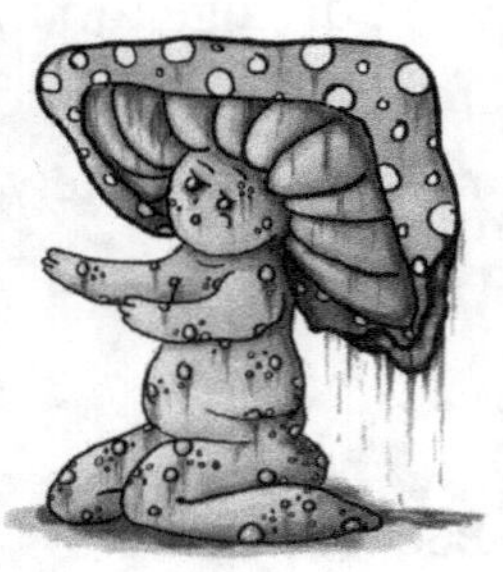

Assorted Illustrations from
Human Scars on Planet Skin
by Effie Joe Stock & Nathaniel Luscombe

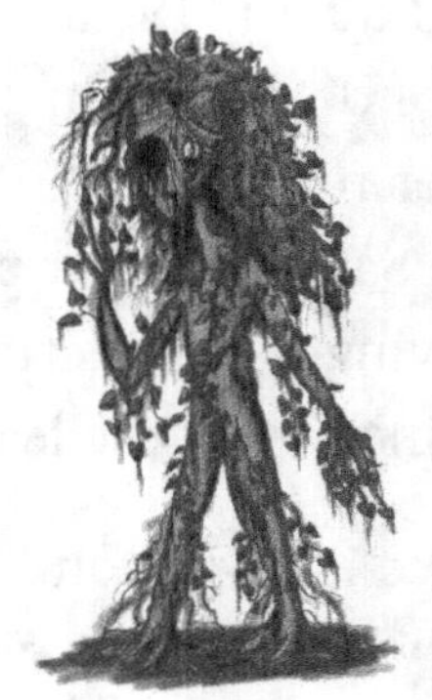

My Last Day
on Earth
By Glen Weatherhead

Threads, X, and Instagram:
@GlenWeatherhead
Or www.CreativeWritingWizard.com.

Glen Weatherhead is a fantasy author, known for his published fantasy short, "Foray Into the Blood Tree Forest" and romantic fantasy short, "The Letter from Leif". He is also known in the writing community for founding Creative Writing Wizard, which supports, encourages, and provides resources for writers and aspiring authors. His Indie Release Radar has supported hundreds of authors as they release their books and was shortlisted for the London Book Fair - 2025 Trailblazer award. He is writing a high fantasy novel and a romantic fantasy novella.

I feel the weight of my bed pushing back at me as I slowly open my eyes. It's morning, but only a small amount of light creeps in through the window. I blink and feel my mind waking up. Something feels different—a weight on my chest draws my eyes downwards. Instead of the child I expect to see sitting on my chest with bedhead hair and eyes filled with expectant wonder, I find myself face to face with a small fairy standing on my ribs. His face is slightly more rounded than the fairy tales I grew up with, and it looks like he has a bit of patchy stubble.

Clearing his throat, this fairy informs me, in a deep gravelly voice, "Hey bub, just so you know, your ticket is getting punched today so… Ya know, get your affairs in order and whatever."

Befuddled by the appearance of this small creature and what he just said, I ask, "I'm sorry, what?"

I wipe the sleep from my eyes and take a few more blinks to make sure I'm seeing clearly.

"You know, ticket punched? Sand runs out?" the little fairy says, his face scrunching up as his tone grows more annoyed.

I sit up, still confused, causing the small fairy to jump off my chest. He flutters his wings before landing next to me.

Finding it difficult to stand steady on the bed, the fairy says more forcefully, "You've got one more day to live. This time tomorrow it's off to twinkle town… You know the afterlife?"

"Oh…" I reply, but I'm still stunned by this new information and with the messenger who delivered it.

"I'll be back this time tomorrow," he says, waving a small wand in his hand, before mumbling under his breath, "humans…"

With a fizzle and a pop, the small fairy disappears, and I'm left alone.

For a moment, I sit in silence as my waking mind tries to catch up with the information. I take a breath in and the words catch up to me. I'm hit with a sudden wave of emotion—confusion mixed with shock. Under all this emotion is a current of energy.

"Well, if this is my last day on earth, I've got things to do!" I say as I hoist myself out of bed and reach for a pad of paper and a pen, "time to make a list!"

I write across the top of the page, Last Day on Earth: To Do, then write the number one.

"Number one," I say as I write, "fold the laundry…"

I pause for a second, No… Scratch that, I think, and cross it off.

I write the number one again, but I'm stumped.

Nothing comes to mind, and I really begin to wonder what is left after I'm gone. I sit in the silence of my sleeping home, pen and pad in hand. I look over to my wife, still sleeping, and out the door to my daughter's room.

"All our plans for the future… we were going to go to Enchanted Land theme park next year," I say and trail off.

Then it dawns on me, why not go today? I can figure out what to do on the way there.

I wake up my wife and daughter and say, "We're going to Enchanted Land!"

Understandably, they're confused as to this sudden rush of energy and the change of our plans on a whim. This is especially odd for me, but my young daughter is already filling a backpack with her favorite stuffies as my wife tries to match my sudden gusto.

I ask my wife to drive, which is not that uncommon coming from me. Normally, I'd ask so I could work on business emails and organize meetings. Not today. I've got something much more important on my mind, something I can leave behind when I'm gone. Along the way I write for my young daughter.

I start with the heading, How to be a Good Person.

I scratch that out and think for a second… I know! I write, How to Make Lots of Money.

Nope, Scratch that. Who knew writing would be so tough?

I sit with my thoughts and I look out the window of our car as we drive along the highway. I see farms that have been growing crops for many generations and I think about how their ancestors have left these fields as a part of their legacy.

Then it comes to me.

I start a new page, and at the top I write, How to Live a Life That Truly Matters.

We pull up to the airport and park in the long term parking. I surprise my wife when I say it doesn't matter the cost. Pulling my little family along with a quickened step, I approach the ticket agent and I buy three tickets for the first flight to Enchanted Land.

My daughter pulls on my shirt, asking to 'boop' my credit card on the machine and pay. I'm trying to focus on what the ticket agent is saying, and so I absentmindedly shoo my daughter away.

We almost make it through security without any issues, until my daughter decides to run ahead and draws the attention of all the security guards. I jump out of line to bring her back, apologizing profusely for the disturbance. The heat in my neck is slowly fading when we finally arrive at our gate, 30 minutes till boarding.

I set our carry-on bags down and pull out my pad of paper. Writing as it comes to me, I continue jotting down words of wisdom I want to pass on to my daughter after I'm gone. While I'm writing, she dances around and ducks under the metal railing, giggling all the while.

"Look at me, Daddy!" she says gleefully as she performs her tenth pirouette.

"Uh huh," I say, not looking up.

"Did you see? Did you see?"

"Yeah, good job baby girl," I say, as I write another nugget of wisdom that just popped into my head.

We finally board the plane, but not even 10 minutes into the flight my daughter knocks over her water onto my notepad, smearing some of my words.

"Gah! This is important," I say.

My daughter shies away, "Sorry, Daddy."

"It's fine," I say after a deep breath, "just be more careful."

The rest of the flight is uneventful and we make it to the gates of Enchanted Land. My daughter perks up as we approach. I catch her sight for a moment and see the look of wonder glistening in her eyes.

On a nearby fence post, I see the small fairy from this morning. The fairy eyes me, tapping his wrist as if to tap a watch, then he disappears again. My family doesn't seem to notice and I rush them through the entrance to Enchanted Land.

At once, we're off. We only have one day to do as much as we can, and somehow in between it all, to write these words for my daughter. I try to find every opportunity I can to write down my thoughts. Some thoughts come easily, and yet other times I'm finding it difficult to focus with the loud noises of the theme park around me.

My daughter rides the Kiddie Dragon for the fifth time. I stand nearby and jot down a few more thoughts that come to me. Passively, I hear the sound of her laughter over the noise of the chaotic fun around me. It's all so distracting.

I feel a sudden pain in my shin and look down past my pad of paper to see my daughter kicking me.

"You're mean!" she says as she kicks me again.

"Hey!" I say, trying to protect myself from further kicks, "we're in Enchanted Land, aren't we?"

"Come on a ride with me, Daddy!"

"I'm doing something important—go on without me."

She turns, but I see her expression droop. Her arms drop to her sides for a moment before she picks up her pace and joins her newfound friends.

I feel a pang of regret as the image of her sad eyes burn into my mind. Shaking my head, I remind myself that what I'm doing by writing down these words of wisdom is more important and long-lasting. She'll have these words long after I'm gone, so I need to write down as much as I can!

After writing a few more points down on my notepad, I take a moment to look up and ponder what else to write. In doing so, I notice another small fairy sitting next to a parent across from me. This one seems to be indicating to the parent that their time is also running out, but the parent couldn't be bothered. Instead, the parent is sitting on the ground with their son and playing in the dirt with a few toys.

Intrigued, I walk over and introduce myself. The parent smiles back at me, and then continues playing with their son.

I ask, "This might sound like an odd question, but do you also see the fairy sitting next to you?"

The parent turns to look at the fairy, then back at me, "Oh, you see it too? That's neat."

"Not sure if that's the word I would use…"

"Your last day on earth too, eh?" the parent says to me.

They toss a toy to their son who giggles and smashes it into another toy he is holding.

"So it would seem."

The pair continue to play on the ground, and after another moment, I feel a sense of frustration rising up in me and ask, "Shouldn't you be doing something more important with your time?"

"Hmm? Oh, yes. Well, I knew my son always wanted to come to Enchanted Land, so here we are!"

"I see… Well, I'm writing down a list of all the important things I want my daughter to know," I say, holding up the notepad.

"That's nice," the parent says and smiles at me before yet again continuing to play with their son on the ground.

I walk back to where I was sitting before, somewhat perplexed, and continue writing down more thoughts. My wife sits next to me and clears her throat. I continue to write, and so she clears her throat again, seemingly to signal that she wants my attention. With a sigh, I look up from my notepad.

She looks at me, and with a still and calm voice, says, "Murdoch, you've been looking at your notepad quite a lot."

"Yes I know. It's important," I say, but I don't know how to tell her why.

"Mhmm. Well, it made sense on the drive because you normally work then. And on the flight, there wasn't much to do. But you're missing out here."

"I know it might be hard to believe right now, but what I'm doing is really important. Rest-of-life, kind of important. It's for our daughter," I say, slightly tilting the pad towards her.

"Yes, well, so is coming here. Those notes may be important, I don't know. But what I do know is that she is important. What do you want her to remember of her time here?" she says to me, with a nod to our daughter playing with other children.

Taking a moment to catch her breath, my daughter looks up at me with a glimmer of whimsy in her eyes and a smile. But as I look at her, an image flashes in my mind of the sad expression she had from before. My mind fast-forwards through time to see this moment from her perspective. Her last memories of me would be sitting here with notepad in hand, writing away.

A sensation like a cool stream washes over my insides as tears start to well up in my eyes. I put down my pad of paper on the bench and walk towards my daughter. With quick last steps, as she turns to see me, I pick her up in a bear hug and spin her around. Tears leak from my face as she hugs me back and we spin.

The rest of the afternoon I spend every moment I can with her. I ride alongside her on all the rides, share a large ice cream cone with way too many scoops, and laugh with her as we watch costumed characters perform.

All the way home, my daughter can't stop talking about the amazing things she saw and replays the moments we had. She somehow finds a way to talk through the entire flight and every step back to our car. It isn't until we strap her into her booster seat that she finally conks out and falls asleep.

My wife puts her hand out to me as I drive with a look of gratitude in her eyes. I take her hand in mine as we sit quietly together listening to music.

We tuck our daughter in when we get home and turn to go to sleep ourselves. I still have the notepad, but I leave it by the bedside. I pull out a separate piece of paper and start writing a note to my wife. In all the activity, I couldn't find a way to tell her about the fairy and what was going on. Struggling to keep my eyes open, I start to write a last letter to my wife. Before I realize it, I fall asleep.

Suddenly I wake up with a familiar weight on my chest. My heart races, The letter to my wife is only partially finished!

"Hold on," I say to the gruff looking fairy, "let me finish this letter."

"Sorry, bub. When it's your time, it's your time."

"Can't you give me an extra two minutes? Does it make that much of a difference?"

With a grunt, the gruff fairy crosses his arms, "Look, Greg, these things aren't decided by me. I'm just here to enforce it. We fairies pride ourselves on precision and process. Don't make it more difficult than it has to be."

He uncrosses his arms and starts to prepare some sort of spell as his little wand glows.

Then his words hit my mind as my brain catches up to what he just said, "Wait, hold on!"

"What now?" the fairy rolls his eyes, lowering his wand.

"What did you call me?"

"Huh?"

"Just now, what did you call me?"

"Greg. What of it?"

"That's not my name!" I almost shout, smiling.

"Huh?" he says with a scrunched-up face. He pulls a small piece of paper from his tiny pocket, "It says right here, Greg Shellock, living at 42 Rosewood Lane."

He turns the small paper towards me, which I squint at—it's written in some fairy language I can't comprehend.

I correct him, "My name is Murdoch. Murdoch Williams. And this house is 42 Rosewood Way."

The fairy looks at the paper again, then with a sigh, "You humans and your street naming conventions."

He puts the paper back into his pocket and turns away, waving his wand.

"Hold up," I say, stopping him once again, "so, today is not my last day?"

"Seems not," the fairy says and then mumbles, "I'm never hearing the end of this back in HQ…"

A fizzle and pop, and the gruff fairy poofs and disappears, leaving me with a giant grin on my face.

I see my pad lying next to the bed and I pick it up to write something, but then decide to run to my daughter's room. It's still early morning, so she's still sleeping, gently snoring away.

Looking down at the notepad and all the words I wrote for her, I take out my pen and write one final line, Spend time making memories with those you love.

Putting my pad down, I sit next to my daughter in the quiet of the morning. I brush the hair from her face and think back on all the fun we had together. In this moment, I promise myself to remember this lesson that the fairy unintentionally taught me.

I rest my hand on her little arm, feeling her breathing rise and fall. Covering my mouth with my other hand, I begin to cry—thankful.

Cargo
by Floyd Largent

I'm a former archaeologist who never woke a sleeping god or uncovered any ancient evils (alas). I'm currently a full-time write and editor. I've recently published or had accepted for publication short stories in Altered Reality, Bullet Points, Bewildering Stores, Androids and Dragons, Black Petals, and Corner Bar Magazine.

Let's see now — what's it like to be one of the people who proved conclusively that humanity's not alone in the universe? . . . Where the hell do you people get these questions?

Wait, wait. I'm sorry. I'll tell you. The truth is, it sucks.

Yeah, I'll talk to you. Don't act so surprised. I'm drunk, I'm sick of the secrecy, and this'll bloody well save me from being just a tiny little footnote in a textbook somewhere. Weinstatter doesn't deserve all the glory. I'm the one who made the real discovery, you know.

No, not the one you're thinking of.

Back when I was in grad school, they taught us that the Great Sphinx was basically a prettified yardang — an elongated erosional feature made of solid rock. Add a head and legs, carve a few features, lop off the nose (we have Napoleon's troops and a cannon to thank for that, by the way), and viola, you've got one of the Eight Wonders of the Ancient World.

Well, it was a good guess.

So far, I've avoided talking about the Sphinx and what we found there. No nine-figure deals for me, no adulation, no product endorsements. When most people ask, I say I get fulfillment enough just knowing I was part of the team that made life better for all of humanity. I've been afraid to say anything else, anything at all, for fear that I'd spill what I promised not to. But I'm nearing the end of my fifteen minutes of fame, so I thought I'd better say my piece about the Gangwasi artifact while people still care.

You know the backstory: a few years ago, Herr Doktor Weinstatter was poring over gravitational differential maps recorded by the Egyptian government, when he spotted it: an unusually large mascon — mass concentration — anomaly centered on the Sphinx. It was exactly the sort of thing he was looking for. See, the denser an object is, the more it affects the local gravitational field. Really dense objects, like chunks of metal, cause a tiny but detectable spike. Less-dense objects and underground cavities produce a different signature. It was the latter he was looking for, and the Sphinx paid off in spades. Weinstatter was so excited he almost wet his pants. He was absolutely certain he'd found the burial chamber of some heretofore unknown king, and he couldn't wait to get his chubby little Prussian hands on it.

I won't bore you with the details of the years of struggle he went through to obtain the funding and permissions he needed to mount an excavation — he did that himself in his book. Suffice it to say that, by this time last year he and several tons of equipment were in Egypt, and I, his top graduate student and heir-apparent, was there with him as crew chief. Lucky for him — there aren't too many archeology grad students who have degrees in Computer Science.

The Egyptian government was pretty excited about it too, but they weren't willing to noticeably damage one of their top cash cows, so they made us build a wood-timbered tunnel that dipped more than four meters under the sand and butted against the long-buried side of the monument. That took us twelve days. Once we'd finished the tunnel, we were required to very carefully carve a replaceable entrance no more than two meters on a side. Jackhammer time. We started that on the thirteenth day, and were going great guns until we struck metal the next morning, about a meter below the surface of the rock.

Not just any metal, either: it turned out to be a titanium alloy, twenty centimeters thick and shiny as the day it was made. It wasn't Egyptian by any stretch of the imagination. At no time did the ancient Egyptians ever have the capacity to work any metal harder than bronze. Our first reaction was disappointment. Obviously, the material was modern. We'd been duped. We just started packing it in, ready to go home in disgrace.

But Weinstatter couldn't leave it alone. He kept bleating about how there was no way anyone could have hoaxed us; there was absolutely no evidence of any of seam or joint on any part of the monument's body that we could see, either below ground or above it. The head and legs, sure. They'd been added later. But the stone comprising the bulk of the Sphinx was all of a piece. And you know, he was right. He had me half-convinced before the day was out.

Then we got back the potassium-argon dates for the rock we'd removed from the Sphinx's side as we excavated, and I was completely convinced. According to the University of Cairo, the carbonaceous basalt was about six million years old, give or take a few thousand years. Kind of young for a yardang, sure. The strontium-rubidium dates we got from UCLA a week later confirmed the K-Ar dates. By then, it was clear the Sphinx wasn't a yardang and never had been. The samples had been collected from locations thirty to eighty centimeters below the Sphinx's surface, and there was no evidence that they were intrusive or that they'd ever been disturbed from their current position. Further study proved that there was no discontinuity where the rock and metal met; the titanium just graded into solid basalt. It was like nothing we humans have ever built.

We burned our way through the metal skin with oxyacetylene torches, and before we were half done it was clear that something wonderful and unprecedented was on the other side, because breathable air was filtering through and we could see light through the cutlines. We broke through at 1237 GMT on September 23 last year, and Weinstatter made a point of being the first person through the portal.

I'll never forget it. He turned to look back at us, his eyes filled with wonder, and promptly fainted. I shoved Weinstatter aside and followed him in. Then I turned around, ran back to camp, called the authorities, and the rest is history.

The films you've seen don't do it justice. The ship is just massive, so big it puts any of our own spacecraft to shame, and it's still fully operational, even after all this time. The cool-fusion reactor still works, and will apparently continue to do so for millions of years more. We named the people who built it "Gangwasi" — not for any logical reason, but for a stupid one. I stumbled on the threshold when I passed through the portal the second time, and I grabbed at a green pillar to steady myself. We still haven't decided if it's a piece of equipment or statuary or even some sort of burglar alarm, but whatever it is, when I touched it a deep tone rang out and a gargling whisper croaked something that sounded like "gang-wa-si." It's still whispering the same word, over and over. Probably it means something like "Hands Off!," but whatever it means, the name stuck.

I lived in that ship for eight days before the UN troops hustled me out, having claimed the derelict for the good of humanity, and Weinstatter was there beside me the whole time. I'm not sure if I ate at all during that period. I do know that at the end of it, I was a good five kilos lighter than when I went in. By then, we'd explored every centimeter of the place we could find access to. Every bit was clean, well-lighted, perfectly ventilated, and pleasing to the eye, even the cargo holds and engine compartments.

I'd say the ship's at least as big as the Queen Elizabeth II, maybe bigger; the bit that's visible is like the visible part of an iceberg. Most of it's underground. The rock on the outside, as it turned out, was just a cheap form of radiation shielding that had somehow been spun out of the fabric of the ship's skin. By the way, we did finally find the airlock. It's located 30 meters below the surface, but it's standing open, so we figure something got out alive when the ship crashed.

It's the find of the millennium sure enough, the most important thing human beings have ever discovered, and I still have nightmares about it every single night. I can't deny that the Gangwasi ship has been a godsend; it's brought humanity together in a manner unprecedented in our history, and it's kicked our technological evolution ahead by several centuries. The CF reactor alone will impact human civilization more than all the inventions of the nineteenth and twentieth centuries combined. But, despite the UN Accord, not everything we found on the ship has been shared with everyone.

Weinstatter has announced publicly that the Gangwasi ship was a wayward freighter, a cargo vessel that for some reason wandered into our solar system and crashed, and he's telling the truth about that. But when he says he doesn't know what the ship was carrying, he's lying through his teeth.

We have no idea what happened to the pilot, or what he might have looked like, or even if there was one. The computer system is fantastically complex. But we do know what happened to the cargo. In each of the eighteen cargo bays, 20,736 empty plastic cubbies are racked in neat rows reaching to the ceiling. Apparently they popped open when the ship was stranded, releasing their contents. The interior of each cubby is specially molded to accommodate a small four-limbed shape.

Now, I'm from Arkansas. Those neatly-stacked containers reminded me right away of something I saw every time I used to get out on the highway.

Ever get stuck behind a chicken truck? One of those flat-bed semis loaded with hundreds of metal pallets, each of which contains a dozen drawers, with a fryer stuffed into each? The Gangwasi cargo bay was like that. It puzzled us at first, until I cracked the computer system and found the manifest. It was written in a language we may never translate, but it was accompanied by a visual record that clearly showed the cargo being onloaded, and helpfully provided specs for several typical cargo units.

Once he'd fully absorbed the import of what we'd found, it took Weinstatter about thirty seconds to order me to erase the manifest and all related files. I did my best, but there are probably still traces of 'em in there. He swore me to secrecy, and until now I've kept quiet. Sure, Weinstatter may be right. Maybe this particular truth isn't healthy for the species. I didn't agree then, and I don't now. I think it should be shouted from the rooftops. We need to be prepared, just in case. Because I've developed a new theory about what the glowing green pillar is: I think it's a distress beacon, which had malfunctioned and failed to activate — until I touched it. Now it's working fine, thanks to me.

So what? So this: we recognized the cargo. Any anthropologist would — hell, you're a science writer, you'd probably recognize them too. They were australopithecines. Great granddaddy a half-million generations removed, to you and me. And it's obvious they weren't passengers.

That's why I no longer sleep well. That's why I worry every single goddamned day. What happens if the Gangwasi detect the distress beacon's broadcast, after all this time?

And what if they come looking for their wayward chicken truck?

THE END

Resources

Find the Freelancer You and Your Book Need

Artists/Designers

CaffeinateArt

I create character illustrations for book covers and marketing material with a specialty in the fantasy genre.

Instagram: @CaffeinateArt

Kate Korsak
Fantasy Cartographer

hiiiii my name is kate and I make fantasy maps! I'm an indie author who got into fantasy cartography as a way to bring my own worlds to life. I found that I loved creating new worlds and mapping them, and eventually decided to offer cutsom maps to other worldbuilders!

I make maps for: authors, homebrew RPGs, any fantasy world you want mapped!
please be sure to read the terms before commissioning me!!

Website: ko-fi.com/katekorsak
Instagram: @writerkatek

Bethany Pardoe Art

I am a mainly traditional artist and illustrator passionate about fantastical, narrative-based projects such as book covers, children's book illustrations, spot illustrations, and hand-lettered font. If you are looking for a vibrant and expressive illustration to bring your project to life, I would love to be involved!

Website: https://btp2101.wixsite.com/bethany-pardoe-art
Instagram: @bethanypardoeart

Rose Everille

Hi, I'm Rose, and I'm a freelance artist! I'm open for commissions, and as a writer myself, I love bringing characters to life. I also have experience with illustration and am open to other projects. Some of my favorite themes are decay and overgrowth, celestial bodies, religious imagery, and anything historical. Some artists that inspire me are: Devin Elle Kurtz, the pre-raphaelites, and Ireen Chau.

Instagram: @rose_everille_writes
Email Inquiry: rose.everdeen.author@gmail.com

Character belongs to beabubb. Art by me.
Posted with permission.

MoonPress Design

Hello! I'm Bianca and I'm a book cover designer based in Atlanta, GA. As a professional cover designer, I've been able to work with bestselling authors, publishing houses and indie authors on a variety of different projects and genres. Being able to connect and work with professionals in the writing industry is one of the best parts of the cover design business! I specialize in creating designs for covers that meet their expectations as well as the current market standard.

Instagram: @moonpressdesign

Sakura Artist

Amelia • 28 • Freelance Illustrator
Co-Creator of @ahcomicmagic
Illustrator for 'The Safekeepers' on Webtoons

Website: https://linktr.ee/Sakuraartist
Instagram: @sakuraartist

Marketing/Development

Through The Faerie Lens

I offer professional book marketing photos, where you ship me your book and I create styled, high-quality images perfect for social media, websites, and promo. I also provide Discord ARC team and street team management, setting up and organizing servers, tracking sign-ups, and keeping readers engaged so authors can focus on writing. On top of that, I offer beta and alpha reading services (specializing in romantasy), giving detailed, thoughtful feedback on plot, pacing, character development, and reader engagement to help strengthen your story before publication.

Instagram: @throughthefaerielens

Small Press/Publications

BEYOND THE STARS PRESS

Beyond the Stars Press is a small indie press, specializing in speculative fiction and poetry with a prioritized interest for own voices stories from POC and disabled authors. We also offer editorial services, and are constantly curating a list of resources for indie authors, as well as free tips and tricks to help others in the industry.

Instragram: @beyondthestarspress
Website:
seraamoroso.com/beyond-the-stars-press

THE FRUIT SLICE

Fruitslice is a Queer-run quarterly publication featuring work exclusively by Queer creators. We platform marginalized voices, especially BIPOC, Disabled, and Trans creators who are overlooked by mainstream outlets. Curated in real-time from across the Queer diaspora, each issue is a cultural document that reflects and shapes the movements, language, and dreams of our communities. It's both a snapshot of our collective present and groundwork for a Queer Future.

Website: https://thefruitslice.com/
Instagram: @thefruitslice

Wanderlust Publishing

Wanderlust Publishing was founded in 2025 by Ashley Ingebrigtson. She grew up with a passion for books and stories, and when it came time to decide how she would make that passion into her career, Wanderlust was born. We are a small, traditional press aiming to publish amazing stories, helping our authors tell their stories the right way (AKA, THEIR way) and helping readers travel to new worlds with every turn of a page.

Wanderlust's goal is to keep creating and providing those worlds for readers to travel to, all while working closely with authors to bring those worlds to life.

Website: https://www.wanderlustpublishing.com/
Instagram: @wanderlustpublishing

Editors

Olivia J. Bennett – Wordshaker Editorial

Olivia J. Bennett offers fiction editing and book coaching services for indie authors through Wordshaker Editorial. Specializing in contemporary and speculative fiction in young and new adult age brackets, she loves working with titles that are genre-bending, fresh, and emotional. As a certified English teacher, she has a unique blend of writing and teaching skills to identify each writer's obstacles and present practical solutions in her book-coaching sessions. Her favorite part of editing is getting to be an author's biggest cheerleader, helping them realize their literary dreams. Check out her website for her editorial portfolio, sample edits, and lesson plans!

Website: bit.ly/oliviajbennett
Email: oliviajthewordshaker@gmail.com
Instagram: @olivia.j.creates

Ink and Industry

I do developmental edits on YA novels in the sci-fi & fantasy genres.

I will read through the manuscript and provide a developmental edit letter with areas to improve. This may include character development, pacing, structure, and worldbuilding information. Included is one Zoom call to discuss and clarify the letter. Note: this is NOT a proofreading edit, this is a structural edit. I'm not looking for your typos and commas, but your character arcs and pacing. I will help you place your story beats, not your apostrophes.

Website:www.inkandindustry.com

Sterling Hooker Editorial

As a freelance editor with four years experience with small and mid-sized publishers, Sterling Hooker brings both technical knowledge and emotional connection to the editorial process. She specializes in developmental editing for story, content, and theme as well as copyediting in Chicago style. As a creative writer herself, she approaches her freelance work with an editor's brian and writer's heart. She views editing as a puzzle, one best solved by understanding the author's unique publishing goals, writing style, and story. Reach out to her for a free thirty-minute call to talk about what editorial stage is right for you!

Website: https://www.sterlingmz.com/

Mendell Studios

I. Love. What. I. Do. Working with authors to help them bring their stories to life is a true joy— and I do my very best to ensure that my authors feel my joy throughout the project!
Not only will you have my utmost respect, commitment to the craft of writing, technical prowess, and extensive expertise in character development, but you'll have a new friend with whom you'll complete the journey. Let's write together!
Editor & Copywriter || fantasy, Christian fiction, and nonfiction/theology || Developmental edits || Line & copy edits|| Theological development

Website: www.mendellstudios.com
Instagram: @mendellstudios

Editor H. A. Pruitt

Website contact page:
https://www.hapruitt.com/contact

I provide editing services for authors working on their manuscripts. For $0.008 per word, I provide developmental editing, content editing, copyediting, and proofreading (two rounds of editing). I am open to all genres except horror and erotica, and I am open to hard topics but will not accept manuscripts with excessive cursing, sexual content, or gore. If you have any questions, please ask.

Promotionals

Looking to Support Small/Indie Authors?

**Promotions are sent in by individual authors and as such are not directly endorsed by Dragon Bone Publishing ™ **

THE KEYHOLDER'S APPRENTICE
BY DEREK M CARTWRIGHT

Four friends. One portal. Zero clue.

After a drunken night out, Celia, Paul, and Sarah stumble through a portal to the World of Rock. Johnny chickens out until he sobers up and follows, only to find that one Earth day equals a year over there. Oops.

The World of Rock is dying, the gods are literal rock stars, and their fans are losing their souls (and not in a musical way).

Cue jetpacks, vampire banshees, a telepathic keyholder, drag royalty, witches, a duelling Austen cosplay court, and a Pride parade versus a death-metal apocalypse.

Johnny's just trying to find his mates but he might accidentally save the world.

Website: www.derekmcartwright.co.uk

SANDED SOUL
BY TORI DIEDERICH LUNDELL

A harsh punishment is cast upon Morpheus, the god of dreams, by the Night Council. He caused an imbalance in the world and must now roam the earth endlessly as the Sandman. Placing his sanded palm over the eyes of those who sleep, he brings dreams to all who have lost hope during WWII.

Klara, an unexpected visitor from Germany, is somehow able to enter his dreamworld, breaking the lonely chains that bind him.

They must find a way to battle the evil that taints the existence of humanity.

Drawn into an adventure of fairy tales and nightmares come true, two very different hearts must work together to face unimaginable horrors.

Buy Now on Most Major Online Retailers

Away From Grace
by Jess Autiero

The Archangel Michael had one mission: to stop Lucifer from escaping Hell. He failed.

Trapped in a young human body, stripped of his immortality and angelic powers, Michael faces a new life he never wanted. Finding small joys in his new existence, he vows to avoid angelic wars at all costs—until a tragedy forces him to reconsider his promise.

As chaos brews and haunting dreams grip him, will Michael have the courage to protect humankind once again? And when his deepest love is his greatest enemy, will he be able to confront the creature he cherishes above all?

Instagram: @autierowrites
Buy Now on Amazon & Kobo

Element
the Graphic Novel Series
by Brittany Leonard

Luna's anxiety and depression are getting worse, and her roommate Jay wants to help. When the two escape the city for nature, they're unexpectedly transported to Elemental Dimensions—Air, Water, Earth, and Fire—each with unique climates and dangers. Separated in this strange world, they must reunite and find a way home. But with each new portal, the mysteries deepen: a ruined city, endless night, and mythical threats. As they uncover what's really going on, Luna and Jay must decide—should they leave this world untouched, or risk everything to change it?

Instagram: @authorbrittanyleonard
Website: Authorbrittanyleonard.com

Living with the Season:
Summer Wellness
by Brittany Leonard

Discover the season of summer in a whole new way. This wellness booklet invites you to slow down and embrace the warmth, energy, and vibrancy of the season with mindful activities, journal prompts, and inspiring quotes. Enjoy nourishing seasonal recipes, complete with zero-waste kitchen tips, and reconnect with nature through simple, intentional living. Whether you're seeking balance, creativity, or deeper appreciation for the summer months, this guide will help you align your wellness journey with the rhythm of the season.

Instagram: @authorbrittanyleonard
Website: Authorbrittanyleonard.com

The Ice Moves for No One
by Arlo Z. Graves

Selkie Warrior Aalgur Thalon was born to fight in honor of the Dread One but when her own body betrays her, Thalon realizes no training or battles have prepared her for what comes next.

Nothing in this world bends easily. The odds are stacked against her, and the path ahead is nothing but locked doors and closed fists. But Thalon has never let anyone—man, woman, or god—decide her fate.

Instagram: @arlozgraves
Website: www.arlozgraves.com

All (Dead) Girls Lie
by Piper L. White

A new sapphic YA thriller for fans of Heathers and A Good Girl's Guide to Murder.

Sixteen-year-old Quinn is a liar, but she isn't a murderer. When the sleepy town of Boiling Springs, North Carolina is roused by the murder of a local teen, Quinn is thrust into a life of danger, disrupting her normally unnotice-able existence. As Quinn becomes romantically involved with Gilly, the best friend of the dead girl and daughter of the town sheriff, the situation becomes even more complicated.

Instagram: @piperlwhite
Website: piperwhitewrites.com

The Vein Severed
by Estelle Tudor

Lady Roselle Lamont faced an impossible choice. Torn between the life of her twin sister, or new husband Lorcan's freedom, she paid the ultimate price of 100 years of punishment.

With the century drawing to a close, Roselle resigns herself to retribution while clinging to the last vestiges of humanity. When Lorcan discovers her on route to London, summoned by their punisher, Roselle must prove her love while plotting out revenge.

Together, they must decide who to trust in the dark and twisted dance of Court politics if they are to ensure survival and any hope of a future.

Instagram: @estelle_tudor_author
Buy Now on Amazon

THE SCION CONSPIRACY
BY MIKE CAHOON

During a burgeoning Age of Exploration, a conspiracy of deadly politics and dark magic is conspiring to abduct children from across the continent for an unknown purpose. As the greatest powers in the world fight for control over the New World, alliances shift by the moment and no one's future is set in stone. As goes the Conspiracy, so goes the world as nations are dragged along in its wake, forever defining all that follows in the first installment of this dark fantasy epic.

By Now on Amazon
Website: www.mikecahoon.com

LONELY FOREST
BY DARBY S. FISHER

Every tree has a shadow...

Pollux has never been beyond the yard. Outside the safety of home lies the endless forest — a cluster of trees that conceals beings of evil. Or so his parents say. But Pollux longs to breathe in the mysteries lurking beneath the boughs.

Finally bold enough to seize his chance, Pollux races towards the trees, eager to discover their secrets. But when he is bewitched by a doll who takes him to Mother — a power-hungry witch eager to make him into a drone — he must fight not just for his freedom, but for his very existence.

Buy Now on Amazon

TORSION
BY SERA AMOROSO

Torsion (noun). the state of being twisted.

Nine students are invited to attend Torsion University, a prestigious, and mysterious school, known for its technological advances. Every person has something to hide, and every person has something to lose. Little do they know that the school's shiny reputation is hiding a secret as well, one that will make or break them. As they work to unravel the web the school has created, they have a choice: Solve the mystery or die trying.

Website: www. seraamoroso.com

The Call of Bones
By M. Sahagun

Rosalind Parker is branded. A mark, seared into her skin, guarantees her services to The Library for the rest of her life. . . . But when a faerie prince comes and steals her away, her entire world shifts. She must battle between two forces competing for the same end: The control of Edryale.
Rosalind must decide to follow her heart or trust what she's been told, in a battle for life or death.
What will her choice be?
Will she save her fated before war breaks out?

Facebook & TikTok: @msahagunauthor

Lights Camera Replay
By A.S. Ishana Balan

What once stood tall as the city's spectacle now lies as an abandoned theatre in the shadowed corners of Oakridge. Except now, it replays your memories.
The sixteen-year-old piano prodigy, Catherine Stanwell, is drawn to the place after mysteriously losing her memories. Torn between finding out who she was and pretending she's still the person she doesn't know, Catherine is exhausted and would do just about anything to get her memories back.
Meanwhile, Aaruni Roy, a fiery website design student with a burning drive to prove herself wants nothing to do with the theatre's games if it gets in the way of work. But in the heat of a moment, she makes one fatal mistake that forces her to play along.
One alliance. Four tasks. All while they untangle their own lives.

Buy Now on Amazon & Notionpress

Liar's Blood
By R. L. Newt

Raised under ruthless dogma, Fyren lives a brutal existence. Her sole aim? Protect her sister. So when the gods mark her sister for death, Fyren takes her place. But her sacrifice goes awry. Fyren wakes among enemies, transformed by their magic. And when she tries to rescue her sister from the cult of their upbringing, those enemies become her captors. Their survival hinges on Fyren, so they're not about to let her go. As new threats arise, and the line between friend and enemy blurs, Fyren realizes that saving her sister will cost her everything. And, it just might tip her world into chaos.

Instagram: @newt_writes_fantasy

www.ingramcontent.com/pod-product-compliance
Lightning Source LLC
Chambersburg PA
CBHW080603300726
48975CB00010B/2781